WILDFIRE

Other Books by Bill Pronzini

The Hangings
Firewind
With an Extreme Burning
Snowbound
The Stalker
Lighthouse (with Marcia Muller)
Games
Freebooty
Dead Run
The Jade Figurine

"Nameless Detective" Novels by Bill Pronzini

The Snatch
The Vanished
Undercurrent
Blowback
Twospot (with Collin Wilcox)
Labyrinth
Hoodwink
Scattershot
Dragonfire
Bindlestiff
Quicksilver
Nightshades
Double (with Marcia Muller)
Bones
Deadfall

Shackles
Jackpot
Breakdown
Quarry
Epitaphs
Demons
Hardcase
Sentinels
Illusions
Boobytrap
Crazybone
Bleeders
Spook

WILDFIRE

Bill Pronzini

SPEAKING VOLUMES, LLC
NAPLES, FLORIDA
2015

WILDFIRE

ISBN 978-1-62815-197-8

This one is for Cathy Pronzini,
Jim Moen and Barbara Norville.

PROLOGUE

From the Miwok County, California, Chamber of Commerce Visitors' Brochure:

Nestled in the county's rugged northeast corner, at the junction of highways 19 and 4, twelve miles above Springwood, is the picturesque hamlet of Logspur. Here the visitor will find a fascinating glimpse both of back-country history and of modern back-country life. During the glory days of logging in the early part of this century, the village was a thriving railhead serving the many small lumbermills and logging camps then operating in northern Miwok County. Today it is the site of one of the oldest independent mills in Northern California, the Johnston Lumber Company. A popular attraction is the old railroad roundhouse, which has been converted into a museum featuring an extensive collection of early railroad and logging memorabilia, including a vintage steam locomotive that is still used occasionally for special summer events.

Surrounding Logspur is a breathtaking wilderness panorama of densely forested ridges and valleys, lush mountain meadows, tiny lakes, and the distant granite peaks of the Trinity Alps. These features, as well as abundant wildlife and the trout-heavy waters of the Miwok River, make the area particularly delightful for nature lovers, backpackers, and sportsmen.

1

From the book *California Today—and Tomorrow*, by Robert Lawrence McGreevy:

Historically, logging in Northern California has been a feverish industry. Every available acre of timber was quickly harvested, at first in accessible valleys and then, with advances in technology, in remote backhill locales. Virgin forest land was thought to be inexhaustible, and most of the smaller companies therefore operated on a transient basis. As soon as a section had been cut and processed, camps were moved to other sections, with no consideration being given to second-growth timber. It was only the large conglomerates which had the foresight and the capital to purchase already harvested land as a long-range investment. As a result, when the supply of virgin timber began to dwindle during the last quarter-century, most of the small mills were gradually forced out of business, and the conglomerates assumed full control of the logging industry.

A few small mills remain operational today, but it seems only a matter of time before they, too, will succumb to economic and ecological pressures. One such mill, the Johnston Lumber Company, located in the village of Logspur in Miwok County, produced in 1960 an average of 500,000 board feet of lumber per day; in 1976 this mill's production had plummeted to slightly under 200,000 board feet per day. Its work force reflects this faltering rate of production: 150 full-time employees in 1960, less than a third of that figure in 1976, with more layoffs expected in the near future.

The effect of the conglomerate takeover of logging and of the slow death of the independent mills is perhaps greatest on the small towns in which their respective employees live. Corporation-owned and -operated "company towns," such as Pacific Lumber's Scotia, in Humboldt County, prosper and flourish; company money provides for inexpensive housing and services, and maintains streets, parks, businesses, schools, and churches. Villages such as Logspur, on the other hand, receive no such subsidy from the struggling independents. They, too, are company towns in the sense that they owe their existence to the mills—their residents are mostly lumber workers and small merchants—but they have not prospered in the Age of the Conglomerate.

Typically, Logspur's population has shrunk steadily from a high of 850 at the turn of the century, when there were several small mills operating in the area, to less than 100 in 1976. Its lone school and four business establishments have ceased operation since 1962; it has no churches, no recreational facilities, save a community hall. Although a county-maintained logging and railroad museum is situated there, the village is too isolated, too poor, too mill-oriented to effectively attract or capitalize on the tourist-and-sportsmen trade.

There can be no doubt, then, that villages such as Logspur will continue to survive only so long as independents such as the Johnston Lumber Company remain operational. When these mills are ultimately forced to shut down, their employees will have no choice except to uproot their families and move elsewhere to find jobs, which in turn will cause the last of the shopkeepers and other merchants to do the same. And the villages, like so many others before them, will become little more than ghosts and memories.

From an Associated Press feature dispatch, datelined September 29, 1977, Miwok County, California:

In this, California's worst fire year since 1923, there have been more than two hundred major forest fires throughout the drought-stricken state. Few counties have escaped the destructive force of a blaze, but one of those is tiny Miwok County, located in the shadows of the Trinity Alps two hundred and fifty miles northeast of San Francisco.

Local residents and forestry officials, however, are afraid that their number may yet come up.

Nearly all of Miwok County is comprised of dense forest land, and it has been five months since rain fell here. Summer temperatures have been high, humidity low. The fuel moisture content of the organic material covering the forest floors—dead wood, brush, dry leaves and needles—is down to 4%, from a normal of 15%.

One forest ranger characterizes the county as "a firetrap." A long-time resident of Springwood, the county seat, says, "Everything is tinder-dry. It's like sitting on top of a pyre, waiting for some damn fool to torch it off."

Allan Carpenter, head of the State Forestry Service office in Springwood, is somewhat less pessimistic. "It's true that we've been lucky so far," he says. "But the fall rains are due pretty soon, and until they come we're all maintaining constant smokewatches."

He pauses. "I'd be lying, though, if I said I wasn't worried. If a blaze gets started around here, as dry as the timberland is, it'll spread with incredible speed. We'll have a wildfire on our hands. . . ."

PART ONE: ASSAULT

ONE

Jim Maxon sat on the edge of his bed, lips peeled in against his teeth, and began the ritual of strapping on his artificial leg.

The thing was made of aluminum, with a thick circlet of foam rubber inside the top, where it fitted over his stump, and a padded harness that fastened around the upper thigh. It didn't look like a leg; it looked like a fancy-designed crutch. Maxon thought of it that way—as a crutch, as something a man who had never leaned on anything or anyone was now forced to lean on for the rest of his life. It was a constant reminder that he was half a man, dependent and sterile, and he hated it. He hated it just as much as he hated the smooth round stump which ended above where the knee ought to be, all that was left of his right leg.

He didn't look at the stump as he strapped on the prosthetic limb; he had stopped looking at it not long after the accident six months before. That made the task of putting on the crutch difficult, but he didn't care about that. He kept his eyes on the open window across the bedroom, fumbling with the harness, getting it cinched into place awkwardly by feel. A thin dry breeze, thick with the smell of pine pitch and resin, came in through the window but did not stir the stagnant air in the room. Even at four o'clock in the afternoon, the Indian summer heat lay like a heavy blanket over Logspur: the temperature was in the eighties.

Pustules of sweat dotted Maxon's narrow, angular face; his T-shirt and shorts were darkly stained with it. He paused to draw an arm across his forehead, to take a long swallow from the can of lukewarm beer on the nightstand. When he finally managed to buckle the harness, he caught the artificial leg in both hands and jammed it hard into the stump, felt a sharp, satisfying cut of pain. Then, in clumsy movements, he pushed up off the bed and stood on one foot and leaned on the crutch. Once he had his balance, he turned and started to the chair where his pants were.

Regina was standing in the bedroom doorway.

Maxon stopped and stared at her. "What the hell are you doing?" he demanded irritably. "You know I don't like you watching me put on the leg."

"I wasn't watching you. I've only been here a second."

"Well? What do you want?"

"Are you getting dressed?"

"That's right."

"I wish you wouldn't."

"Why?"

" I . . . thought we might go to bed together."

"For God's sake. Is screwing all you think about?"

She winced. "Jim, that's unfair."

"Is it?"

"You know it is. It's been more than two months."

"The hell it has."

"It has. Why do you make me beg this way?"

"It's too damned hot," he said.

"You never used to think it was too hot."

"I never used to think a lot of things. I never used to have one leg, either." He looked away from her, limped over to the chair and began to struggle into his pants.

From the doorway Regina watched him. Her eyes were a soft pale gray, like gray velvet—wide, compelling. Maxon avoided them, just as he avoided looking at the stump of his right leg.

She said tentatively, "Jim . . . ?"

"No, damn it," he said. "How come all this sudden need for sex, anyhow? Before the accident you weren't after me about it all the time."

"Before the accident we never went two months without making love."

"Listen, what is it with you? Do you *like* doing it with a one-legged man, is that it? You get off having this stump of mine sliding around on top of you?"

She put a hand to her cheek as if he had slapped her. "My God, what a thing to say!"

"All right," he said. "The hell with it then."

"Your leg has nothing to do with anything between us," Regina said. "Why won't you accept that?"

But she was lying; he knew that. Wordlessly he finished zipping up his pants and pulled his damp T-shirt off and replaced it with a thin cotton pullover. Then he clumped into the bathroom, ran cold water into the sink.

Regina came over to stand in that doorway. He glanced around at her, and his gaze lingered briefly on her small gamin face and the lock of natural blonde hair that curled down over her forehead. On the tight-fitting shorts she wore, the brown willowy flatness of her stomach, the sheen of perspiration on the upper swells of her breasts where the halter top dipped loosely. A faint stirring of desire came to him—

but then he thought about his stump, and the desire guttered and died.

He looked away from her again. Washed his face, toweled it dry, and ran a comb through his kinky black hair. Thick beard bristles made his cheeks look shadowed, made him look ten years older than thirty-one. The hell with that too.

"I suppose you're going out," Regina said.

"Yeah. I'm going out."

"Down to The Tavern again?"

"What difference does it make?"

"I wish you wouldn't drink so much—"

"What the hell else is there to do?" he asked bitterly. "Watch crap on television? Stare at the walls? Listen to you talk about screwing?"

"We could *talk*," she said. "That's another thing we haven't done in a long time."

"Talk about what?"

"What we're going to do."

"Do?"

"Yes. We can't live on your disability pension from the state, you know that. And you throw a tantrum every time I mention getting a job—"

"Don't start that again, Regina."

"All right, then. Are you going to change your mind about taking that job in the railroad dispatcher's office in Eureka?"

"I already told you—no."

"It's a good job—"

"It's a lousy job," Maxon said.

"Why? Because it's office work?"

"That's right. I'm not going to sit behind some goddamn desk all day, shuffling papers. I couldn't stand it."

"Jim, be realistic. What other options do you have?"

"I'll get a tin cup," he said savagely, "and beg nickels on a street corner. That's all a one-legged man is fit to do, right?"

"Won't you ever stop feeling sorry for yourself?"

He glared at her. "Feeling sorry for myself? Jesus Christ, that's all I need to hear from you."

"I'm sorry, Jim, but it's the truth. Can't you—"

"It's bullshit," Maxon said, and pushed past her roughly and stalked across the bedroom, down the hall, through the small living room, to the cottage's front door. He heard Regina following him, but he didn't look back at her. He caught the handle on the screen door, jerked the door open, and limped out onto the porch and started down the steps.

But he was too angry to pay attention to what he was doing. The "foot" on the artificial leg caught on one of the lower treads and sent him sprawling onto the stone path at the bottom.

He landed painfully on his hip and left elbow, rolled half onto his back. Above and behind him Regina said, "Jim!" and there was the slap of the door as she came out. She ran down the steps, started to bend over him with her hand extended.

A black rage had control of him now; he slapped her hand aside. "Leave me alone!" he shouted at her. "Get the hell away from me!"

She flinched, backed up a step. Maxon struggled into a sitting position, got his good leg under him and managed to heave himself erect. In one of the evergreens that flanked the cottage to the south, a jay made a raucous cry, as if it were laughing at him. He could feel his face flaming. He balled his fist and slammed it against the prosthetic leg, slammed it into the stump. Again. And again.

"Jim, don't—"

He pivoted away from her, hobbled down the path to the front gate. On the dirt surface of Spruce Road beyond he stood staring through a dusty haze of sunlight and tree shadows at the village center three blocks away. Bastard, he thought. Bastard! And drove his fist once more into the stump of his right leg.

TWO

When Steve Hannigan came down the east slope from his homestead cabin and crossed the rail yard, he saw old Ed Staggers sitting on one of the shaded benches in front of the roundhouse. Hannigan veered over toward him. Staggers was industriously polishing a brass whistle knob with a soft cloth; the cold nub of what had once been a cigar protruded like a wart from one corner of his mouth. At Hannigan's approach, he glanced up and a smile creased his wrinkled hound face.

"Afternoon, Steve."

"Ed." Hannigan sat down beside him.

"Glad you stopped by. Haven't had much company today."

"No museum visitors?"

"One family. Never much business, this time of year."

Hannigan stretched his long legs out in front of him and mopped perspiration from his face with his handkerchief. He was a loose-limbed man in his early thirties, three inches over six feet, with shaggy red hair and gentle brown eyes. His hands were huge, blunt-fingered, heavily callused; combined with the weathered texture of his face, they told you that he spent a good deal of his time working outdoors.

Staggers said, "You just stop to shoot the breeze, or you need something else for your book?"

"Just to talk, Ed."

"Book coming along all right?"

"Not as well as I'd like it to."

"How come?"

"The heat, I guess," Hannigan lied.

"Know what you mean. It kind of dries up a man's brain, after a while."

Hannigan nodded and looked across Mill Street and the oak-shaded green which fronted the roundhouse to the west. On the far side of the park, the buildings along the one-block Main Street—Evans Texaco, Logspur General Store, The Tavern, the two empty storefronts, the Rec Hall—sat baking in the glare of the sun. There was not much traffic of any kind. The houses and cottages to the south, where all of the village residents lived, looked equally somnolent. The only signs of activity came from the Johnston Lumber Company, several hundred yards to the north, where the only two roads into Logspur intersected: County Highway 19, angling down from the northwest, and County Highway 4, angling down from the northeast, creating a wide pie slice with the mill in the bottom center of the slice. Logging trucks streamed along both roads, passed up and down the mill's access road and in and out through the main gates of the compound. Ragged columns and stream-

11

ers of white smoke from the kiln stacks drifted across the sky, caught in faint crosscurrents of the hot afternoon breeze.

Staggers asked, "You line up a publisher yet, Steve?"

"Finally. A small house in Los Angeles."

"How come a small one?"

"None of the big ones would bite."

"Hell. Lots of interest in trains these days."

"Sure. But a history of short-line railroading in Northern California doesn't have mass-market appeal—or so I was told at least a dozen times."

"Mass-market appeal," Staggers said. "Crap."

Hannigan shrugged. "Publishing is big business these days, Ed. Unless you've got a property with potentially large sales and a profit margin, you have trouble placing it."

"Must be tough on you writers, then."

"Sometimes. I never did think commercially myself, so I've been hungry a time or two in the past eight years."

"That the reason you left San Francisco and came up here to homestead?"

"Part of the reason," Hannigan said. "I don't like cities much, and I've been into whole-earth ecology for years—wrote a couple of articles on woodbutchering and the back-to-nature lifestyle. So I decided I ought to go ahead and do it myself, finally."

"You must like solitude, all right, living back there on the ridge all alone."

"I like it," Hannigan said.

"Couldn't do it, myself," Staggers said. "Always did need people around me. And a woman in my bed. Domestic type, that's me."

Hannigan was silent. A woman in my bed, he thought, and felt his stomach knotting again. That was the way it had been lately. So many things reminded him of her, and with every reminder there came a physical reaction inside him. He had stopped lying to himself weeks ago: he was in love with her. Sometimes he imagined she had at least some similar feelings toward him, because of the way she looked at him whenever they met, the sad shy way she smiled at him. Other times, he believed she did not care for him at all, that in his own ardor he was mistaking friendliness for affection.

He didn't know what to do. He wanted to force the issue, find out the truth—but she was married, and to a man who had lost a leg only six months ago. How do you force the issue in a situation like that? Do you really want to?

"Go for a cold beer at The Tavern, Steve?" Staggers asked.

Hannigan roused himself. "Yeah, I could," he said. "You closing up early?"

"Might as well."

They stood and went inside the roundhouse. The interior was cavernous and orderly and clean; the whitewashed walls, swept floors, trusses, and engine pits gleamed under the roof lights. Ed Staggers was an old logging and railroad man and he took his retirement job as custodian of the roundhouse museum seriously.

Along the walls were tool bins and tool racks and workbenches and glass-fronted cases containing historical photographs, small equipment of different types, other railroad and logging mementoes. On the turntable at the far end was the fifty-year-old 1500-

horsepower Baldwin 4-8-4 steam locomotive the county had bought at auction twenty years ago, when the North State short-line road folded, which Staggers kept in immaculate condition. This past July, as he did every year, he had hooked up the steamer to the old passenger coach and the converted caboose on the siding outside and taken most of Logspur's citizens over to the county fair in Springwood.

Hannigan remembered that day well and thought about it again now in spite of himself, as he followed Staggers across to the locomotive. He had sat next to Regina both ways on the trip, because her husband had not gone along, and they had eaten lunch together at the fair. It was the longest time he had ever spent with her. It was the day he had known he was in love with her.

Staggers climbed up into the cab, carrying the polished whistle knob. Hannigan stood below and watched him replace it. Over on one of the workbenches, a portable radio tuned to the Springwood station crackled with the voice of a newscaster. Hannigan paid attention when the newscaster said that a fire was raging up at Pine Hill, thirty miles to the northeast, out of Miwok County, and had already destroyed more than two thousand acres of timberland. Air tankers had been called in with fire-retarding chemicals, but it was not yet under control. Forestry officials were cautiously optimistic that they would be able to contain it within the next twelve hours.

Staggers had been listening, too, up in the cab. He said, "They'd better contain it in the next twelve hours. Fire like that spreads to five thousand acres, it'll be too damn wild to tame."

Hannigan nodded.

"Christ, what a year," Staggers said. He swung down off the locomotive. "Drought, heat, dry timber—we've been plenty lucky not to have had a fire start up around here."

"I guess we have," Hannigan agreed.

Staggers moved over to shut off the radio and then went to the big engine doors beyond the turntable. They were open partway, and when Hannigan came up beside the old man he could see through to where two sealed boxcars sat on the Springwood spur tracks outside. He had noticed them when he crossed the yard earlier.

"What's in the boxcars, Ed?"

"Machine parts, supposed to be."

"Supposed to be?"

"Two boxcars is a hell of a lot of machine parts."

"Are they being shipped out?"

"Yep. Down to Los Angeles, according to Ben Kiley. He brought 'em out on the yard engine a couple of hours ago. SP's sending up for 'em tomorrow morning."

"Why would the mill be sending two carloads of machine parts to Los Angeles?"

"Exactly what I asked Ben," Staggers said. "He didn't know. Said Johnston had the cars loaded last night from a storage shed up at the mill that's always kept under lock and key. None of the workers were allowed inside, and he can't recall any of the parts ever coming in or ever being used. Kind of funny, you've got to admit."

"A little," Hannigan said. He helped Staggers slide the doors shut and lock them down. "I've heard talk that the mill is losing money."

"Sure. Independent mill can't compete with the big

15

combines these days. Folks around here won't admit it, but they're scared spitless Johnston will decide to close up."

"Well, maybe he's selling off some kind of stock equipment in order to raise capital."

"Maybe. But he's a queer bird. Always did play things close to the vest, and since his wife died a few years back he doesn't talk to anybody around here. Spends part of his time traveling to Christ knows where and the rest of his time locked inside that house of his inside the mill compound. Hell, he could have any damn thing at all in those boxcars."

Hannigan shrugged. "Whatever's in them, I guess it doesn't really concern us."

"No," Staggers agreed as he led the way back across the roundhouse to where the light switches were located. "I guess it doesn't, at that."

THREE

In the pine-paneled office on the second floor of his house, Henry Johnston said into the telephone, "Believe me, Warren, the decision to ship by rail instead of by truck is the right one. It's faster and it's safer."

"I wish you'd consulted me first," the voice on the other end in Los Angeles said. "Who loaded the cars? Tell me that."

"I assigned a crew here at the mill."

"Damn it, Henry, what if one of them got curious—"

"My men don't get curious," Johnston said. "They don't dare; they value their jobs too highly for that. Besides, I supervised the loading myself."

"Somebody could have dropped a crate, broken it open—"

"But no one did."

"Well, I still don't like it," the voice in Los Angeles said. "What if there should be a derailment? What if a railroad inspector somewhere wants a look inside those crates?"

"There's not going to be a derailment," Johnston said patiently. "And there's no reason in the world why a railroad inspector would want to look at a consignment of machine parts. There's nothing to worry about, Warren. There's nothing that can go wrong."

A pause. Then Warren said, "All right. All right. But if our friends in Florida don't get the shipment, the consequences will be on your head."

"Noted and accepted."

"All right," Warren said again. "When will the cars leave Logspur?"

"Ten o'clock tomorrow morning."

"What's their route?"

"From here to L.A., then straight across country and down into Florida. They should arrive in five days. I've already made arrangements for them to be left on an industrial siding outside Tampa. Our friends can unload them there by truck."

"You'll forward the particulars?"

"Of course. Later today by phone."

"Call me if there are any problems."

"There won't be any problems."

"I hope not. Goodbye for now, Henry."

"Goodbye, Warren."

Johnston replaced the receiver and sat smiling at it. But there was no humor in the smile; his dark-amber eyes were bright and cold. He was a small bony man in his mid-fifties, with brush-cut hair peppered with gray and lips so thin they were like an incision across the lower half of his face. A long, narrow neck gave him an attentive look, as though he were perpetually craning it to watch and listen.

At length he shook a cigarette out of the package on his desk, lighted it, spun his chair around to the picture window in the outer wall, and rested one foot comfortably on the sill. From there he could see most of the mill compound spread out below—the sawmill, sheds, and storage buildings; the stacks of logs and cut lumber and the conical mounds of sawdust; the cranes, trucks, rail tracks, and yard engine; the workers moving here and there at their jobs. Another hour until quitting time. Then nearly everything would be shut down and the compound would be deserted except for the skeleton night crew. Not like the old days, when full crews worked in eight-hour shifts around the clock. But, then, nothing was like it was in the old days. Nothing. Nothing.

Johnston smoked and let his gaze roam beyond the mill, over the village and the evergreen-carpeted slopes which surrounded it. As always, the overview made him feel somewhat like a feudal lord surveying his fief—because Logspur *was* his; he owned it and controlled it; without him it would cease to exist. But he took no satisfaction in the fact. Here he had power, yes, and here there was cleanliness and godliness; but Logspur was an infinitesimal speck on the globe. Outside its boundaries there was moral pollution and ideological and spiritual corruption, there was filth and decay and chaos. And he had no control over it, no power to change it immediately and directly.

Still, the situation was far from hopeless. As long as there were such men as himself and Warren and the people in Florida, working together, fighting together, there was hope for the world. In their unity was the power they lacked individually, and it was growing stronger all the time, and someday—someday—they would be powerful enough to seize control by ballot as well as by force. Then the filth and the corruption would be wiped out, and there would be cleanliness and godliness everywhere, as there once had been.

On the tracks behind the roundhouse Johnston could see the two sealed boxcars, waiting to make their cross-country journey to Florida. He thought about what was in them and what it would be used for, and he smiled again, grimly this time. The shipment would get through without any difficulty, all right, because it *had* to get through; the Caribbean maneuver was a vital step in the overall scheme of things. Warren's concern was groundless.

After all, what could possibly go wrong?

FOUR

The big truck-and-double-trailer rig with the words *Hammond Freight Lines* stenciled on all three pieces drifted along Interstate Highway 5 south of Redding at a steady forty-five miles per hour. In the cab Mel Zacharias sat slouched down on the passenger side of the seat, one foot anchored against the dash. Like the heavy-set black man behind the wheel, he was wearing dark glasses and Levi's and a blue chambray work shirt; a khaki cap covered most of his curly brown hair.

He said, breaking a five-minute silence, "Nice country up here."

"Yeah," Vernon Frame said.

"Hot, though. Hot and dry."

"Yeah."

"What's the matter? Don't you like the great outdoors?"

"I been better places."

"Trouble with you, boy, you're a city boy."

Frame gave him a sharp sidewise look. Sweat glistened on his boxlike face and smoothly shaved head. "Knock off that 'boy' shit, Mel. You know I don't like that shit."

Zacharias grinned. He got a boot out of needling Frame once in a while with racial barbs; it always got a rise out of him, because he was sensitive about the color thing. But Zacharias didn't mean anything by it, and Frame knew that. They had worked together off and on for years and were pretty good friends. He had even fixed Frame up with a white woman once, in Vegas—big-titted knockout white woman who got off on making it with blacks. Christ, what a week that had been. He'd won sixteen hundred dollars on the crap table and scored with two different girls in one of the shows. But that was before he'd gotten married to Lila and settled down and had the kid. Now he went home to the house in L.A. after every job and celebrated by puttering around with the sailboat he was building. Funny how a man's lifestyle could change completely like that, how all of a sudden he enjoyed doing things that would have bored him silly a few years ago.

Frame put his eyes back on the road and asked, "How much farther to this Springwood?"

"Another seventy miles or so."

"Be dark when we get there."

"Good."

"We going in tonight, right?"

"Depends on what Tully has to tell us. And how things look."

"Yeah," Frame said. He rubbed moisture from his thick mustache with the back of one hand. "You sure this is clean action, Mel?"

"I'm sure."

"It still sounds heavy to me. A lumbermill is a hell of a place to stockpile munitions."

"It's a good place," Zacharias said. "Who'd figure it?"

"Ordnance worth a quarter of a million bucks, and this guy Johnston keeps it locked up in a storage shed. No guards, nothing but a couple of dogs. Man, it just sounds too good to be true."

"Nobody knows it's there except Johnston," Zacharias said. "He bought it all on the sly over the past several months, small truckloads at a time coming in late at night. It's just supplies, as far as the mill workers are concerned. Besides, Tully says he runs the place like a prison camp—fences all around, watchmen on the gates that don't let anybody in without clearance. He puts guards on the ordnance, all he does is call attention to it, and the workers start getting curious."

21

"None of them ever got curious anyway, huh?"

"No. Johnston pays good money, and they're all afraid of their jobs. He's a little tin god; they don't buck him, they don't get curious, they just do what they're told."

"I still say there's got to be some kind of catch."

"No catch, Verne."

"Then how come this cat that tipped you didn't put a hijack together himself? How come he's willing to settle for ten percent?"

"I already told you," Zacharias said. "He works for the people who supplied the ordnance; he doesn't want anything to do with a strike or selling off the goods afterward. Word gets back to his people that he's ripping off a customer, they make him dead."

"Why's he trust you?"

"Because I worked a job with him once, six years ago, and he knows I always keep my mouth shut. And I know you keep yours shut, and so does Tully. All right?"

"Yeah," Frame said, "I guess so."

"All right."

"But what about this Johnston dude?"

"What about him?"

"He's got to be crazy, stockpiling weapons and ammo that way."

"Sure, he's crazy. So what?"

"No telling what a crazy man will do," Frame said. "Go up against a crazy man, any damned thing can happen."

"Jesus, will you quit worrying? We'll handle him."

Frame didn't say anything.

"Why're you so uptight, anyhow?" Zacharias asked him. "I never saw you so jumpy before a job."

"I never been in on this kind of strike before."

"The big time too much for you, baby?"

"It ain't that and you know it."

"What is it, then?"

"I need bread, that's all. I'm tapped; I can't afford to lose out on any job right now."

"You won't lose out."

"Yeah," Frame said. "Yeah."

Zacharias shook his head and wondered if Frame's nervousness was going to carry over to the strike. But no, Verne was too much of a pro for that. Good man, one of the best. Tully too, even if he was kind of a flake. Besides, you couldn't blame Verne for getting excited; thirty percent of a quarter of a million dollars was enough to make anybody excited. Hell, he was a little keyed up himself, he had to admit it.

He shifted position, scratched at the cleft in his lean chin—Lila said the cleft made him look like Kirk Douglas; that was a laugh—and looked out through the windshield. Heat mirages shimmered on the highway, and the sun glare reflecting off passing cars was intense, at times momentarily blinding even with his dark glasses. The sky to the west was fiery; it made the pines on the rocky hills look as though they were silhouetted against a wall of flame. Nice country, all right, he thought. He'd have to bring Lila up here sometime. She'd like it here.

He said, "So what're you going to do with your share, Verne?"

"Head for Vegas; what else?"

"Always Vegas. No wonder you've got to work so often."

"I crave action; that's my nature."

"You ever think about getting married, settling down?"

"Not me. One woman ain't enough for me."

"You'll change your mind when you meet the right one."

"Man, they *all* the right one, you dig?"

Zacharias laughed. "You know something, Verne?"

"What's that?"

"You're okay—for a nigger."

Frame's eyes flashed. "Mel, goddamn it . . ."

"Well, you are," Zacharias said, and punched him lightly on the shoulder. "You worry too damned much, but you're okay. I may even fix you up with another white woman one of these days."

FIVE

Regina Maxon carried the small portable fan into the cottage living room from the kitchen, where she had finished preparing another dinner—meat loaf, this time—that she would have to eat alone. She plugged it into a wall socket near the writing desk and stood in front of the whirring blades for a moment, letting the draft dry some of the perspiration on her body. But the fan was not very powerful, and as soon as she stepped away from it and sat down at the desk, the hot dusty air enfolded her again and brought out a fresh sheen of moisture.

She picked up the letter from her sister in San Diego which had arrived the day before, read through it another time. Then she took a tablet and a pen from the center drawer—and sat staring at the blank white paper, trying to arrange her thoughts. At length she put down the date, hesitated, and finally began to write.

Dear Ellen,

Received your letter of the 24th. It's wonderful news that you're expecting again. I know how much you and Don want a girl. You sound so happy and things are going so well for you, I hate to burden you with my troubles. But I just don't know what to do and I need your advice. Desperately.

Ellen, my marriage is dying. I don't know if I can save it, or even if I want to save it, God help me. Jim has changed so much since the accident, you can't imagine what it's done to him and what he's doing to himself. He's so full of self-pity it's like a cancer eating him up inside. He won't accept the job in Eureka, he won't plan for the future, he won't do anything except lie around the house all day and drink at the local tavern at night. He refuses to talk to me and he hasn't touched me in two months. He just doesn't care about anything any more and I'm afraid he never will again.

It's so obvious that he doesn't love me now. I wonder sometimes if he ever did—I mean deeply, the way I loved him when we were married six years ago. And the truth is, Ellen, I don't think I love him any more either. It's not just the way he's changed, the self-pity and the rest of it. I wouldn't admit it to myself but we were starting to grow apart even before the accident. I understand that now.

And yet I don't know if I have the courage to divorce him or even if a divorce is the right thing to do. It might feed his self-pity and make things even worse for him. I feel guilty every time I think about it, it's like I would be betraying him.

Regina turned to a third clean page of the tablet, hesitated again. Outside the living room window the two

Bennett kids had begun bouncing a rubber ball off the side of their house next door; the steady thump, thump, thump of the ball and their shouts and laughter echoed through the fading afternoon. Inside the room, except for the humming of the fan, it was breathlessly still.

She tugged at the sweat-damp crotch of her shorts, spread her legs out wider on the chair to keep the material from chafing her thighs. She was not at all sure she wanted to go on with the letter. Maybe it would be better if she phoned Ellen. Yes—but a long-distance call was so expensive, and it would be even more difficult to say these words over a telephone wire. Knowing Ellen, she would probably call when she got the letter. They could talk then; it might be a little easier then.

Reluctantly Regina bent once more to the tablet.

> There's another thing on my mind I'd better tell you about because it makes matters even more complicated. Another man. No, I'm not having an affair, it's nothing like that. We're just good friends. But he'd like us to be much more than that. He's never said so but I can tell, you can always tell. And I think I'd like us to be more than that too. His name is Steve Hannigan and he's a writer who lives in a homestead cabin near here.

The pen felt slick in her fingers; she laid it down and reread what she had written about Steve Hannigan. It seemed foolish and awkward, like something a teen-ager would write about a boy she had a crush on. Regina tore the sheet off the tablet, crumpled it and started to toss it into the wastebasket. Then she changed her mind, got up and carried the paper into the bathroom and flushed it down the toilet.

She stood watching the water swirl in the bottom of the bowl. Steve Hannigan remained in her thoughts, as he often did, and she felt guilty and selfish, as if by thinking about him that way she were betraying Jim, committing a form of adultery. The rational part of her mind rejected that, insisted she was only looking for normalcy and another chance at happiness and love, but the emotional part would not release her from her commitment to Jim. If their marriage was intolerable now, who was to say it would not get better if she kept on waiting and kept on trying? If she felt a strong attraction for Steve Hannigan, who was to say it was not simply a groping reaction to the events of the past six months—that it was sexual and perverse, nothing more than a self-serving means of escape?

She simply could not decide what was true and what was right. All she knew for certain was that she had to make a decision one way or another, and that it had to be made soon.

When the toilet's flush mechanism was still, Regina returned to the living room and sat down again at the desk. She couldn't tell Ellen about Steve Hannigan, at least not yet, not in this letter. Ellen would understand—but it was something she had to work out alone, in her own mind, and it must not have anything to do with whether or not she decided to leave Jim.

She picked up the pen and wrote instead:

> There isn't any easy answer, I know that. But I just can't keep it inside me any longer, I've got to have help making up my mind what to do. You've always been the strong one in the family, Ellen, and I trust your advice and I need it. I can't go on this way much longer.
>
> Love to you and Don and the boys.

Regina signed her name, addressed an envelope, and immediately folded the letter without reading it over and sealed it inside. In the bedroom she put on a thin shirt over her halter top. Then she left the cottage, hurried along Spruce Road to mail the letter in the post office in Irv Norcross's General Store.

Before she could change her mind about mailing it at all.

SIX

The Tavern was deserted except for Al Logan, the owner, when Jim Maxon got there and claimed his customary table by the front window. Then Ed Staggers and that homesteader, Hannigan, came in, and later Burt Evans, and then the full shift at the mill had ended. Now the place was jammed. Maxon preferred it that way, even though he still sat alone at the table and didn't enter into any of the conversations. He had enough emptiness and silence at home; here there was noise, movement, a sense of kinship. He didn't belong any more, and yet he did. They all pitied him, he hated their pity and their pretense that nothing had changed, but he was still one of them.

It wasn't much, but it was all he had left.

He drank from his fifth stein of beer, stared out through the window at the mill compound in the distance. Twelve years, he thought, twelve years. The only job he'd ever had except for the summers he'd spent with his father working on the old steam switch engine in the Eureka rail yards. A friend of his father's had gotten him on at the mill right after he graduated from high school. Yard laborer, saw filer, planer—right up the promotion ladder to assistant foreman on Ben Kiley's rail crew. Right up the ladder to the day one of the crane lines broke as they were loading cut logs onto the flatcar and a rolling log caught him and crushed his leg, crushed his future along with it.

Twelve years. He was a mill worker, a railroad worker; he didn't know how to be anything else; he didn't want to be anything else. Now he was nothing. Half a man, a cripple, a one-legged gimp with a lousy disability pension and a lot of empty memories. Useless. Shit, useless. It would have been better if that log had landed on his head, put him out of his misery right then and there.

Maxon pulled his gaze away from the window, lit a cigarette and blew smoke at one of the old logging prints that shared the walls with mounted deer heads and trophy-sized antlers. There was not much else in there except for the long bar and the tables and a couple of wood-frame booths along the back wall. The floor was usually carpeted with sawdust, but Al Logan had stopped putting it down during the early part of the summer, as a precaution against fire. No jukebox, none of that crap—this was a company man's tavern. You wanted dancing and socializing with wives and girl friends, you went down to the Rec Hall on Friday and Saturday nights, or over to Springwood.

Dancing at the Rec Hall. Yeah. Before the accident he'd taken Regina down there two or three weekends a month, they'd danced for hours; everybody said how light on his feet he was. He'd taken her hiking then, too, back in the hills where the Miwok River ran, and they'd bowled one night a week in a mixed-doubles league in Springwood. All that was gone, too. What good was he to Regina now? He couldn't do anything for her; he couldn't even screw her any more.

But she wasn't much good to him, either. Always talking about building a new life, always pretending like everybody else that things weren't as bad as they seemed. Harping at him, pitying him. Maybe it would be better for both of them if she moved out and left him alone, got a divorce. He might be able to live alone on the disability pension; the two of them sure as Christ couldn't do it. So what the hell did he need her around for?

Conversation and laughter rose and fell around him. He was sealed off from it, but he listened anyway. Ed Staggers holding forth about a highballing run he'd once made through a snowstorm in the High Sierra, when he was a relief engineer on a short-line logging road. Joe Linscott and Burt Evans and Lee Adcock talking about the fire up at Pine Hill, how the Forestry people said they expected to control it before morning, but how chances didn't look good they'd be able to do it. Sam Baker and a couple of the other men rapping about the day's work at the mill. Bud Franklin telling a joke that broke up Lloyd Tyrell. Maxon wanted to join in, but he had nothing to say, nothing to contribute. He'd tried it at first, after he got out of the hospital, and it had been awkward and painful—everybody uncomfortable, conversations dying, pity beating at him like waves. So he'd given it up, let them know he didn't want anything more from them than to sit alone in their midst. He didn't need them individually any more than he needed Regina. He didn't need any damned body at all.

Maxon finished his beer, shifted around on his chair to wave the empty glass at Al Logan behind the plank. He shouted above the din, "Another beer, Al." Logan saw him, motioned that he'd heard.

When he swung back he saw the homesteader, Hannigan, get up from his chair next to Ed Staggers and make his way over. Shit. Hannigan stopped beside the empty chair opposite, offered a tentative smile.

"Hello, Jim," he said.

Irritably Maxon scowled at him.

"Thought you might like some company."

"Yeah? Well, you thought wrong."

Hannigan hesitated. "Buy you a beer?"

"I don't take charity."

"Buying a beer isn't charity—"

"I'll pay for my own."

Again Hannigan hesitated. His eyes were solemn—like Regina's eyes, like all of their eyes when they looked at him. Big bastard, quiet and easygoing, but tough in his own way. Self-sufficient. Even though he was an outsider, the others liked him and accepted him. Maxon didn't like him at all. The pity was one reason, but the main one was that Hannigan had the hots for Regina.

You'd have to be blind not to see it in the way he looked at her. And maybe she was interested in him, too, judging from the way she looked back at him sometimes. There wasn't anything going on between them—Maxon would have known about it if there had

31

been, because Regina was no good at lying to him—but there might be if he was out of the picture. Thinking about that possibility made him see red. Regina and him not being any good to each other was one thing; her going from his bed to the bed of a virile bugger like Hannigan was something else.

"Well?" he said.

"All right," Hannigan said. "Sorry, Jim."

"Sorry? What the hell are you sorry for?"

"Bothering you."

"Then stop doing it."

Hannigan shrugged, turned away. Maxon was aware that Staggers and Linscott and a couple of the others were watching him; he glared at them until they averted their eyes.

Al Logan came over with the fresh stein of beer, set it down. Maxon said, "Wait," and caught up the mug and drained it in a single convulsive swallow. He wiped his mouth, gave the empty stein back to Logan. "Do it again."

"Sure," Logan said. "Sure, Jim."

Maxon looked out the window again. He had to urinate, but he'd wait until everybody went home to their wives and families for supper. He'd wait all night if he had to. He wasn't going to let them see him get up and hobble across to the john on his fucking prosthetic crutch.

SEVEN

It was just seven o'clock when Hannigan got back to his cabin on the ridge a mile above Logspur.

The free-form cabin resembled a somewhat lopsided A-frame, built on sloping ground and bordered closely on three sides by tall pines and Douglas fir. Hannigan had designed and constructed it himself, like other woodbutchers who had rebelled against city living and depersonalized, mass-produced housing. Pieced it together with salvaged lumber, rough-hewn beams, native stone, redwood thatch, and inexpensive plate glass. Furnished it with handmade tables and chairs and bunk bed, and with other necessities gleaned from flea markets and secondhand stores. It suited his needs and reflected his personality; it was his in every respect.

He crossed the old abandoned logging road which wound along the ridge below the cabin, went past his parked ten-year-old Land Rover and up to the curving limb-and-plank stairs. Climbed the stairs to the platform deck and entered the cabin's spacious single room. Evening shadows filled it with the same bluish half-light that was in the forest outside, and he set about lighting each of the three coal-oil camp lanterns. No electricity here, and no plumbing, either. His water came from a small well he had dug on the north side of the homestead; his toilet was an outhouse set well back into the trees to the south. A portable AM-FM radio and the rows of books on crude temporary shelves between his desk and the black stone fireplace gave him all the amusement he needed or wanted.

But tonight the cabin seemed barren and wanting, too quiet. Hannigan switched on the radio, found a station playing country music, and turned up the volume. Then he went to his desk and sat down and looked at the neat stacks of notes and manuscript pages alongside his old Remington typewriter. Read over the last page he had written that afternoon.

Mechanical prose, reflecting a lack of concentration and involvement. He put the page down, rolled a clean sheet of paper into the platen. And sat staring at it with his fingers resting dormant on the keys. His mind was creatively blank. Too much beer at The Tavern and too many other intrusive thoughts, all of them centering on Regina Maxon.

After a while he got up, took a six-ounce can of ravioli and another of mixed vegetables from his larder, put the contents in separate saucepans and the pans on the propane-gas stove to heat. He was not particularly hungry, but making supper gave him something to do for the moment. He set the table with plates and utensils, cut a thick slice from the loaf of bread he had made from ground acorn meal and pine nuts and baked in a clay oven in the fireplace. Stood distractedly stirring the ravioli and the vegetables until they were ready.

While he ate he told himself again that he should not have approached Jim Maxon at The Tavern. Maxon was both Regina's husband and a bitter, angry man who spurned everyone since the mill accident in which he had lost his leg—so what was the sense in trying to hold a conversation with him? Hannigan had done it on impulse, without conscious purpose, and yet it bothered him that he might have had a purpose after all. Such as wanting to convince himself that Maxon, in spite of his handicap, was unworthy of

Regina. Such as looking for a convenient way to rationalize a decision about his own feelings toward her.

He did not want to believe he was that desperate. But maybe he was. He had never been in love before, had never had to cope with emotions as strong as this. He had always shunned personal involvements in the past; his affairs had each been casual and short-lived, calculated to offer no threat to his freedom or his solitude. But now freedom seemed empty and the solitude had become something that approached loneliness, and it was becoming increasingly more difficult for him to function as he had in the past, to do nothing about those emotions. He was not the kind of man who pursued married women—he believed in the sanctity of such conventions as marriage—nor was he unsympathetic toward Maxon and Maxon's plight. But when it came right down to his own peace of mind, his own desires, he suspected he was not selfless enough or charitable enough to do the gentlemanly thing.

Sooner or later, right or wrong, he was going to have to force the issue with Regina.

But what if she failed to respond, turned him away? What then? Would he be strong enough not to pursue her any further? He thought he would be, but he didn't know for sure. He did not want to think about it. The situation was painful enough as it was.

Hannigan finished eating, but only because he didn't believe in wasting food, and then stood and cleared the table and washed the plates and pans and utensils. When he was done with that, he stood in the middle of the room and looked at the row of books. But there was no use in trying to read; he would not be able to concentrate tonight. At length he caught up one of the lanterns, carried it outside and down the stairs and around to the tool shed he had built near the well.

It was dark now. Above the tops of the evergreens a pallid quarter moon hung in the night sky like a pendant surrounded by clusters of stars. The breeze of the afternoon had died, and the air was still, warm, heavy with the scent of resin. Night birds and insects sang intermittently in the forest; a raccoon or other nocturnal animal made a rustling noise in the underbrush nearby. A peaceful night, as were nearly all nights up here.

A lonely night.

Damn it, Hannigan thought. He opened the tool shed, took out the crosscut saw, the plane, the tape measure, several other tools, and brought them over to the sawhorses and the pile of scrap lumber and the half-finished permanent bookshelves. He set the lantern and the tools down, and went to work. Measured, sawed, hammered—trying not to think about Regina.

But it was no use. No use at all.

At the end of forty-five minutes he put the tools away, went back into the cabin and extinguished all the lanterns. Then he came out again, started slowly down across the road and through the trees. He was not going to see Regina; he was only taking a walk, maybe going into the village for another beer at The Tavern—where Jim Maxon would still be sitting, as he sat every night until it closed at eleven. He was not going to see Regina, not tonight, not yet.

Lying to himself all the way down.

EIGHT

When Zacharias and Frame came into Bungalow Ten at the Springwood Motel, Roy Tully was sitting on the bed with a partially field-stripped Thompson submachine gun on his lap and the window beside him wide open.

Zacharias glared at him. "What the fuck are you doing?"

"Jerking off—what does it look like I'm doing?" Tully said. He had a low, scratchy voice, like sand rubbing on glass. "Christ, that's some greeting, Mel."

"Don't you know enough to close the goddamn window and pull the shades? You want somebody to see you with that piece?"

"There's nobody out there," Tully said. "There's nothing but woods out there."

Zacharias went across to the window, slammed it shut and drew the drapes. When he turned, Tully put the sections of the Thompson gun—magazine, buttstock, frame—down on the bed and got on his feet, frowning, looking a little miffed. He was a short, round man who appeared fat but wasn't, who appeared slow and ponderous but wasn't. He had a moon face and fine brown hair that had begun to recede into elongated V's above the temples.

"I took a look around before I sat down with the Thompson, Mel," he said. "Besides, it's too damn hot in here with the window shut."

"We'll open it again when you put the piece away."

"Listen, what're you so nervous about?"

"I'm not nervous. I just don't want anything screwing up this strike, that's all."

"Nothing's going to screw it up."

"Not if we're careful. Careful, Roy."

"Okay, okay."

Zacharias let himself relax. What the hell, no harm done. And no sense in pushing it any further. Worst thing you could have on a job was friction among members of the string; friction led to mistakes. Tully was a flake too—nothing serious, nothing that kept him from being one of the best in the business, but you always had to treat flakes with kid gloves, keep them happy. Like kids.

He put on a smile and said, "Forget it. How's your mother?"

That was the right thing to say because Tully lived with his mother, had lived with her all his life. He was always buying her things and taking her on vacations; she was the only woman for him. And he was the only man for her, too, since Tully's old man had died in a fire when Tully was a boy. Nothing kinky or anything; they just loved each other and preferred to spend their time together instead of with other people. She didn't know what Tully did for a living; she thought he was part owner of a company that bought and restored vintage cars, because that was one of Tully's hobbies. His other hobby was guns, collecting them and sometimes supplying them on a small scale to others in the business. But his mother didn't know anything about that, either.

Tully relaxed, too. He said, "She's fine, Mel. Fine. Be sixty-six in a couple of weeks. I'm taking her on one of those Caribbean cruises."

"She'll like that."

"Sure. Nothing she loves more than traveling." Tully seemed to remember that Frame was there, too, looked over at him. "Hey, Verne. Been a while."

Frame nodded. "How you doing, man?"

"No complaints. You?"

"I'm cool. Been here long?"

"Since four o'clock."

"You go over to the mill?"

"Yeah. Everything looks good."

Zacharias said, "What else'd you bring besides the Tommy?"

"Take a look."

Tully went over to where a suitcase stood open on the luggage rack, took out three bundles wrapped in chamois cloth, laid them on the bed and unwrapped them. The three handguns were Colt Woodsman .22 caliber ten-shot automatics, each one outfitted with a stubby homemade silencer.

"The ammo is hollow point," Tully said. "Hits like a magnum at close range. Okay, Mel?"

Zacharias picked up one of the pieces. He didn't like .22s much because they didn't have any range, and he didn't like silencers because they were undependable, could jam on you. But the Woodsman was a good piece—hell, it was what the Mafia enforcers were using these days—and the silencers were necessary on this kind of job.

He said, "Like always. You know your guns, Roy."

Tully beamed. Just like a kid, Zacharias thought. Damned if he wasn't.

Frame took another of the Woodsmans, bounced it a couple of times in his big hand, and then looked at the field-stripped Thompson gun. He said, "I hope to Christ we don't have to use that bastard. I ain't even so sure it's a good idea to carry it along."

"It's just insurance, baby," Zacharias said.

"Yeah."

Tully said, "Point a Thompson at somebody, he's

not going to give you any trouble. None at all. You know that, Verne."

Frame was silent.

"Hell," Tully said, "you look worried. How come?"

Zacharias said, "He thinks it's too easy. He thinks there might be a catch somewhere."

"What kind of catch?"

"This Johnston's a crazy," Frame said. "Crazies bother me, that's all."

"I checked the place out, Verne, day and night. Went inside the compound once, said I was a contractor looking for an estimate on a load of board lumber. It's easy, all right, but there's no catch."

"All right."

"When we go over there to recon you'll see for yourself."

Zacharias said, "You and I'll go, but Verne stays here."

"The hell," Frame said. "What's the idea?"

"We don't want to take the guns with us yet, and we don't want to leave them here unguarded. That's one reason. But there's a better one."

"What?"

"Use your head. Anybody sees a big black buck like you around that lily-white mill, they're liable to get suspicious."

Frame's jaw tightened. But Zacharias wasn't needling him now, or at least not much. Frame saw that he meant what he said, and saw the sense in it, too. He said, "Yeah, maybe you're right."

"Sure, I'm right."

"So when do we go in?"

"Roy?"

"Anytime after midnight," Tully said. "The town over there, Logspur, closes up tight by then. No traffic, nobody around. There's a skeleton night crew at the mill, but all of the workers are inside the sawmill except for one guy on the gate."

"You got a place picked out for us to go inside?"

"Yeah. And a place to leave the truck."

"Might as well recon right now," Zacharias said. "Give us time to go over the details when we get back."

Tully rewrapped the handguns in chamois, put them away in his suitcase. Then he reassembled the Thompson gun, wrapped that in another piece of chamois. As soon as he laid it on the floor inside the closet, Frame went over to the window and opened the drapes and raised the sash, letting in the dry night breeze again.

Frame said, as Zacharias and Tully started out, "Bring back something to eat, will you? My belly's starting to grumble."

"Sure," Zacharias said. "How about a mess of ribs and a slice of nice cold watermelon?"

"No, man," Frame said thinly. "Honky food's just fine."

Zacharias laughed, and he and Tully went outside and headed across to the graveled parking area where the double-trailer rig and Tully's rebuilt Ford sedan were parked. Tully said, "You shouldn't kid Verne that way, Mel—about him being black."

"He knows I don't mean it. Hell, I'm not prejudiced."

"Sure, but he's sensitive. My mother's the same way about her age. She can't stand it when people call her a Senior Citizen and crap like that. She loses her temper sometimes. Verne's liable to lose his one of these days, too, you know."

"Not with me. We been friends too long."

"I still wish you'd go easy on him."

Zacharias shrugged. "Okay, maybe you're right."

They reached the sedan, slid inside, and Tully took it out of the motel lot and onto the county road. It was muggy inside the car; Zacharias rolled down the passenger window so the hot night air could fan across his face.

Tully began talking about his mother, the cruise he was going to take her on and all the Caribbean islands they would visit. Zacharias closed his eyes, let him talk without interruption. Keep him happy. Keep old Verne happy, too; maybe Tully was right about him using the needle too much. But Christ, what a pair. A sensitive spade and a forty-year-old kid hung up on his mother. Not that he minded too much, though. They were good people and their hang-ups didn't affect them on the job, that was the important thing. And everybody had hang-ups; he had them himself: look at the way he'd changed after he met Lila and got married and had the kid.

A quarter of a million dollars, he thought, and smiled to himself. Oh, baby, who cared about hang-ups? Nobody's hang-ups mattered worth a damn when you were about to score for that kind of bread.

NINE

On the screen in Henry Johnston's darkened study, the flickering images of a naked man and two naked women were having orgiastic sex.

The film was 16-millimeter, in color, complete with soundtrack; the room was filled with the pantings and moanings of the three people on the bed. Alone in there, Johnston sat in a straight-backed chair beside the projector, hands flat on its wooden arms, body stiff with revulsion, and feet planted firmly on the floor. His eyes were fixed on the screen, unblinking.

The movements of the man and the two women, the sounds they were making, became frenzied as the film neared its conclusion. They assumed new positions, even more perverted to Johnston's eyes than any of the previous ones—an incredible tangle of glistening bodies and lust-contorted faces. He did not move as he watched; his body remained rigid, his breathing was slow and regular. There was the taste of bile on the back of his tongue.

The camera moved in on the faces of the women, on the man's genitals, for the last few climactic seconds. There were cries, then sated moans and sighs—and the picture on the screen dissolved into a clean white frame. The room became silent except for the clicking whir of the projector, the faint slapping of film as it wound out of the sprockets.

Johnston continued to sit motionless for several seconds. Then he said aloud, "Filth—God, what *filth*," and got slowly to his feet. He shut off the projector, removed the reel of film and the soundtrack tape. Carried them out of the study and down a dark hallway into the wide, pine-paneled living room.

The embers of a banked fire glowed inside the stone and brick fireplace which comprised the entire west wall. Johnston knelt on the hearth, began to tear the film from the reel. When he had all of it free and mounded in front of him, he laid the empty reel aside, caught up the wormlike pile in both hands and pitched it onto the embers. Broke open the soundtrack tape and tossed that in there, too.

He straightened, stood back as the celluloid caught fire and began to burn high and bright. Orange-rimmed shadows danced across his face; his eyes, still unblinking, reflected the firelight like ovals of black glass. The film and tape burned rapidly, curled, and vanished in the flames. Became ashes that smoldered on the wood embers.

Someday, he thought, we'll burn it all like that—reduce all the filth to ashes. Purity through fire. Salvation through fire.

He released a breath, turned away from the hearth, went to the portable barstand and made himself a light bourbon-and-water. He took the drink to the picture window in the south wall, stood looking out at exactly the same view he commanded from his office upstairs. The mill compound looked deserted now, illuminated by pole lamps and night lights; the village lights were like spots of flame against the sky and the dark forest background. Stillness. Tranquillity. And the twin black shadows of the boxcars sitting behind the roundhouse, waiting.

As he was, as Warren and the people in Florida and all their other allies across the country were—waiting.

But not for long.

Johnston finished his drink, put the glass away. He was tired, but he would not go to bed for another couple of hours. There was still more work to be done tonight, as on every night. Know thine enemies and know them well, the better to destroy them.

He picked up the empty film reel, left the living room and returned to his study. Without turning on the lights he opened the cabinet beneath the built-in bookshelves and at random took out another can of film. Threaded the film through the projector by feel. Switched on the machine.

And sat down again, steeling himself, to watch more of the sickness which had claimed the world.

TEN

Sitting on the front porch swing, in the shadows cast by the old tan oak tree that grew beside the cottage, Regina saw the figure of a man come along Spruce Road and pause outside the gate. At first she couldn't tell who it was, in the darkness; then, when he turned to the gate and opened it, she recognized him.

Steve Hannigan.

She had two distinct reactions, one mental and one physical: surprise and puzzlement, the question *Why has he come here at this time of night?* forming in her mind; and a faint quivering in her stomach, a tightening of body muscles. She watched him walk slowly up the path to the porch and mount the stairs. The shadows hid her from him, and he went ahead to the screen door. Hesitated again, seemed to take a breath, and finally reached out to the doorbell button.

Regina found her voice. "Steve. I'm over here."

His head swung out of profile, and when he had located her she saw a smile appear on his gentle face. He came over to the swing, stopped a few paces away. "I didn't see you in the dark," he said.

"Yes."

45

"Too hot inside the house?"

She nodded. "It's not much better out here."

There was an awkward silence, as if he did not know what to say next. Or as if he knew exactly what he wanted to say and was reluctant to say it. Regina sensed that there was tension in him, a kind of uncertain purpose, and she was suddenly afraid. Of his feelings for her. Of hearing them spoken, being confronted with them. And of herself because she was not ready to deal with any of it yet.

She said, "What is it you want, Steve?"

"A chance to talk to you."

"It's a little late for socializing."

"We have to talk, Regina."

"Talk about what?"

"I think you know."

"No," she said, "I don't know."

Pause. "Is it all right if I sit down?"

No, she thought. And said, "Yes, if you want."

He sat beside her, not touching her, being very careful not to touch her. It was difficult to tell in the darkness, but his face seemed full of conflict. This isn't any easier for him than it is for me, Regina thought. But she intuited that he was going ahead with it anyway. As if he were compelled, driven—and that frightened her all the more.

He said, "What do you think of me?"

"Think of you?"

"Yes. Do you consider me a friend?"

"Of course."

"A close friend?"

She hesitated. "I suppose so."

"Is that all?"

"I don't know what you mean."

"Do you . . . care for me at all?"

She sat stiffly, not responding.

"Regina?"

"I think you'd better leave now," she said, but there was no conviction in the words. She folded her hands together, held them between her bare knees.

"No," he said, "not yet."

He put out a hand, touched her arm with his fingers. The contact sent little shivers through her that were unmistakably sexual; she pulled away—too quickly. "Don't, Steve," she said. "Please."

Hannigan withdrew his hand. "I've got to get this out in the open. I've got to know where I stand."

"No."

"Regina . . ."

"No," she said.

"Do you care for me?"

"No."

"That's not true. I don't think that's true."

"I'm going inside now," she said. "It's late." She started to get up off the swing.

"I'm in love with you, Regina," he said.

She closed her eyes, opened them again, and made it to her feet. Turned away from him and stared past the branches of the oak tree at the sky to the northeast. A faint reddish incandescence tinged the horizon in that direction, like the last lingering afterglow of a sunset. The forest fire at Pine Hill, she thought distractedly. They didn't have it under control yet; it was still raging up there. At night you could always see the glow of a wildfire for miles and miles.

Behind her Hannigan said in a low, difficult voice, "Did you hear me?"

"I don't want to hear you."

"I'm in love with you," he said again.

"I'm married. You know that."

47

"Happily married?"

"Yes."

The lie seemed to hang in the dry hot air, like something tangible that he could recognize for what it was.

"Look at me, Regina."

"No."

"Please look at me."

She didn't move.

The swing's old metal springs squeaked as he stood up. Regina heard him come up behind her, felt him standing there, and she tensed. But when he took hold of her arms, gently, the small tremors moved through her again in spite of herself. She wanted to pull away as she had moments ago, only this time she could not make herself do it.

"I won't have an affair with you," she said, "if that's what you're after."

"It's not what I'm after."

"Then what is?"

"A commitment."

"I already have a commitment."

"But is it what you want?"

"Yes."

"Tell me that face to face."

He released her, backed up a step. Regina's throat felt parched, her face hot and damp; she drew a breath, gathered herself, and turned slowly to look at him. Up close this way, the conflict in his face was more apparent. His eyes, dark-shadowed and steady, locked with hers, and she felt the pull of them immediately, as if his yearning were a kind of magnetic force. They weakened her, stilled the lie she had been about to repeat.

"Regina?"

She heard herself say, "I don't know. I don't know what I want. I need time to think."

"Then you do care for me."

"Maybe I do. I don't know."

"All right. I won't push you any more. I just had to know if there's a chance."

"What if I decide there isn't? What will you do then?"

"I won't embarrass you," he said. "I'll leave you alone."

"Will you?"

"Yes. I won't hurt you, Regina."

"You've already hurt me."

One side of his mouth spasmed, as if with anguish. "I'm sorry—but I had to get it out into the open. I *had* to."

From over at the Bennett house next door, a screen door slammed loudly, and there was the sound of muted voices. Regina jerked her head around, stared over there. Guilt welled up in her, made her back away from Hannigan until her buttocks came up against the porch railing. She listened, looking from him to the darkened front of the Bennett house and back to him again. But the voices remained muted, coming, she realized belatedly, from around back.

"I'd better go now," he said.

"Yes. Please go."

"I won't come again. I'll wait to hear from you."

She shook her head—a meaningless reflex.

"Good night, Regina," he said gravely, and turned and went away from her, down off the porch steps.

She waited until he passed through the gate and started back toward the village center. Then she went inside the house, sat on the sofa in the dark living room. Inside her mind she heard his voice saying the words that Jim had not spoken to her in years, saying them over and over again like an echo that would not diminish: "I'm in love with you, Regina, I'm in love with you, I'm in love with you . . ."

Her hands were trembling.

ELEVEN

Five hundred yards uphill from the Johnston Lumber Company's front gate, Tully cut the Ford's headlights and let the sedan drift off Highway 19 onto a wide dirt turnaround. He braked to a stop, switched off the engine.

"This is where I figured we could leave the truck," he said.

Zacharias nodded. "Not much traffic on the road."

"Hardly any after ten o'clock."

"What about cops—sheriff's patrols?"

"Once or twice a week, that's all."

"Regular days or times?"

"No."

"Suppose a patrol does show up, sees the truck?"

"You mean, would they stop to take a look?"

"That's what I mean."

"They might, but probably not," Tully said. "Lots of big rigs around here, and sometimes a driver comes in late and pulls off on the side to sleep until morning. Chances are they'd pass it right by."

"Yeah, chances are. I don't like that much."

"There's no other place along here to leave the truck, Mel. No place to hide it. You can see that."

"What about the road on the other side of the mill?"

"There's no cover at all over there," Tully said. "Not close to the fence anyway. The sawmill's on that side of the compound, too, and there's a second gate that a set of railroad tracks passes through. No guard on that gate, but the area's pretty well lighted."

"All right, then."

"This is the best place for the truck, believe me. And it's not much of a risk, either."

"All right," Zacharias said again. "Maybe not."

He opened the passenger door, stepped out into the hot darkness. The main gate downslope was partially obscured by trees, as was part of the eight-foot cyclone fence which enclosed the mill compound. The fence ran at a forty-five-degree angle to the road, through high brown grass and thick underbrush; forty yards or so of that rough open ground separated the fence from the turnaround. On the opposite side of the county road a densely forested slope hid the village in the shallow valley below. There were woods behind the clearing on this side, too, extending up around and behind the mill. Lights illuminated most of the compound, but here it was dark, heavily tree-shadowed.

Zacharias walked around the car to the edge of the turnaround nearest the mill fence. Following him, Tully said, "Better not go into that brush. Sounds might alert the dogs."

"How many dogs?"

"Two. Big Dobermans, mean as hell."

"They come right up to the fence when they hear something?"

"Yeah. I went over there a couple of nights ago to make sure."

"Anybody come to investigate the barking?"

"No," Tully said. "No sweat there."

"You sure the fence isn't wired?"

"Positive."

Beyond the fence Zacharias could see a couple of long lean-to arrangements under which were stacks of cut lumber, plywood sheets, and redwood shakes. Night lights glowed there, but the radiance didn't reach as far as the fence.

Zacharias said, "Looks like we can go in right along here."

"That's what I thought, too."

"Ordnance shed's near Johnston's house, right?"

"Right." Tully pointed. "House is up there on the knoll in back; you can see the lights."

"What about the sawmill and the night crew?"

"On the far side of the compound, like I said."

"How far from here?"

"Five hundred yards, maybe."

"How far from the house?"

"About three hundred yards."

Zacharias peered at the house for a time. Big place, two-storied, looked old-fashioned and gingerbready, like one of those Victorian jobs you saw around San Francisco. The upper floor was dark. Three of the windows on the lower level showed light.

"What kind of security on the house?"

"None, as far as I could find out," Tully said. "I couldn't get up there to take a close look. You thinking about an alarm system?"

"Yeah."

"Not much chance of it. Johnston doesn't have any guards on the ordnance, he's got to feel pretty secure inside that compound. Wouldn't be much sense in him putting an alarm system on the house."

Zacharias didn't say anything. He was thinking that Johnston was a fanatic and you never knew what a fanatic might do. But then, it didn't really matter much. If they found an alarm on the house, they'd ring the doorbell and let Johnston open up for them, get inside that way.

At length he said, "He lives there alone, no servants?"

"Just him."

"What about company? Could he have a woman staying over tonight, house guests?"

Tully shook his head. "People I talked to said he's one of these strait-laced types, no women around since his wife died a few years ago, doesn't even seem to like them much. And he doesn't have any relatives left, or any friends, either. Lives up there like a hermit."

Zacharias was satisfied. "Anything else I should know?"

"Nothing I can think of, Mel."

"Okay. Let's go down by the gate."

They returned to the Ford, and Tully drove on down the slope to where the road intersected with the second county highway. At the intersection, bisecting it north and south, another road led to the mill gate a few hundred yards distant on one side, and hooked over to become the main street of Logspur on the other side. The gate was illuminated by pole lamps, and Zacharias could see part of a gatehouse inside the compound. But there was no sign of whoever was on duty there.

Tully said, "You want to go up Highway 4?" Meaning the second county road.

"No. Swing around the village."

Tully slowed, made the turn past a weathered sign that said *Logspur* in two-foot-high redwood letters, and took them over to and along the main street. Buildings on one side, park on the other. All the buildings closed and deserted except for one with a sign on the front that said *The Tavern* and one guy sitting alone at a table in the front window. Couple of people walking around in the park, nobody anywhere on the street. Houses strung out among the trees farther south, a few of them showing light, most of them dark.

"Some town," Zacharias said.

"Real boondocker, all right," Tully agreed. "Another couple of hours, you won't see two lights anywhere."

They circled the square, went past a big wood-and-brick building that fronted a network of railroad tracks. Behind it were two solitary boxcars on the main tracks and a couple of old cars—a passenger coach and what looked like a caboose—on a siding.

Zacharias said, "What's that? A roundhouse?"

"Yeah. This place used to be a logging railhead in the old days. Guy told me they had a whorehouse here then, for the timberjacks. They tore it down when Johnston's old man opened the mill."

"Figures."

Tully grinned. "A fucking shame, Mel, right?"

Which was Tully's idea of a joke, so Zacharias laughed and said, "Right. Right, baby."

When they came back to the intersection Zacharias took another look at the mill gate and the gatehouse inside. He asked Tully, "There a telephone in that gatehouse?"

"I think so."

"Don't *think* so, for Christ's sake. There a phone or not?"

Tully frowned, working his memory. "Yeah, there's a phone," he said finally.

"You sure?"

"I'm sure, Mel."

"You'd better be," Zacharias said. "We get Johnston to call down, tell the gatekeeper to let the truck in, it's a hell of a lot simpler than one of us having to walk him down there so he can give the order in person."

As they neared the intersection again, Zacharias noticed a faint glow in the sky to the northeast. He asked Tully what it was.

"Forest fire," Tully said. "Big bastard, burned three or four thousand acres so far."

There was a kind of sudden tense uneasiness in his voice that made Zacharias say, "How far away?"

"Thirty miles or so."

"Hell, you sounded worried. Thirty miles is a long way."

"I don't like fires," Tully said shortly.

"How come?"

"I just don't like fires, that's all."

Zacharias got it then. The fire that had killed Tully's old man when he was a kid. Smoking in bed, something like that, the father had set himself and the house on fire one night. Tully and his mother had gotten out in time, but he'd been burned a little, still had scars. Scars inside his head too, the way it seemed. Another hang-up. Well, what the hell, he was entitled. Zacharias let the subject drop.

He had Tully stop on the turnaround again so he could get out and make one last recon of the area, see if there was anything else he needed to know. He still didn't like the idea of leaving the truck out there in the open, where a sheriff's patrol could spot it and maybe question what it was doing there. But as Tully had said, there wasn't anything they could do about it—and there wasn't enough of a risk to make him think about calling off the strike. The rest of it looked too good.

They drove straight back to Springwood, stopped at a fast-food place for some take-out hamburgers and coffee, and then returned to the motel and Bungalow Ten. Frame was sitting on one of the chairs with his shirt off and sweat shining like oil on his chest, reading a newspaper he'd gotten somewhere. He put the paper down and stood up as they came in.

"Well? How does it look?"

Zacharias winked at him. "Like a piece of cake," he said.

TWELVE

Al Logan leaned across The Tavern bar. "I'm going to close up pretty soon, Jim," he said. "You want a last round before we call it a night?"

"No," Maxon said without turning his head.

"On the house."

"I said no."

"Sure. Okay."

Maxon stubbed out his last cigarette in the overflowing ashtray in front of him, pressed the heels of his hands to his temples. He'd had a dozen beers tonight and his stomach felt a little queasy and his head ached in a dull, pulsing way. But he wasn't drunk. Tight, sure, but a long way from drunk. That was always the way with him: he'd get tight on five or six, and then, no matter how many he had after that, he never really got shit-faced. Dull his mind, but he couldn't deaden it. Couldn't forget the accident, couldn't forget the stump or the crutch. Hell, just the opposite. More he drank, more he thought about them. Bastards. When he was tight he could almost feel his right leg, too, little twinges in the knee, the ankle, the toes. Ghosts haunting his mind. Dead leg spasming in his memory.

He wondered what they'd done with the leg at the hospital after they'd amputated it. Burned it up in one of those goddamn crematory ovens? Wrapped it up and put it out with the garbage? Dead and gone, whatever—didn't exist any more. Piece of him didn't exist any more. They should have told him what they'd done with the leg. Man had a right to know where a piece of him went. Should have given the leg to him, for that matter. Man had a right to bury his own leg, didn't he?

Hell with it. He looked at his watch, saw that it was 10:40. But he'd already known that. Logan always called the last round at twenty of eleven, set your watch by him. Maxon scraped his chair back, caught his stump in both hands—dug his fingernails into the flesh—and dragged the artificial leg out from under the table. Used the tabletop to lever himself into an upright position. When he glanced toward the bar, Logan was washing glasses in the sink, with his head bowed and his eyes carefully averted. Had to give him that, anyway. He knew better by now than to gawk at a cripple.

"Leaving now," Maxon said briefly.

Logan looked up. "All right, Jim. Good night."

"Yeah."

Maxon waited until Logan lowered his head again, then he hobbled over to the door in slow, careful movements and went outside. The street was empty, and there was nobody in the park, hadn't been for nearly an hour. Townspeople taking walks over there earlier, after supper. Kids playing on the swings and in the bandstand. Kids. Worse than the adults, the way they looked at him: cruelty mixed with pity, laughing at him, making fun of him, behind their staring little faces. Good thing he and Regina hadn't had any kids, good thing he'd been firing blanks the past six years. Living with her was hard enough now; he'd go crazy if he had to put up with a kid all day long.

Because he was tight and a little unsteady on his good leg, he made his way at a deliberate pace along Main Street, past the old schoolhouse that Sam Baker and his wife had bought and converted into a home, to where Spruce Road began. A breeze had come up, blowing down from the north, but it was hot and dry and did nothing much to appease the night's heat. If anything, it combined with the beer he had drunk to draw an oily sweat out of him. He could feel it begin to trickle down along his sides, to chafe his crotch.

When he got to the end of the first block on Spruce Road he saw two men standing at the gate of Ed Staggers' redwood-shingled house up ahead—Staggers and Burt Evans. They played cribbage most nights, but usually they were still at it when he came by on his way home. Now, sure as hell, they stopped talking as he approached and turned to look at him.

"Evening, Jim," Staggers said.

"Evening."

Evans said, "Hot night."

Maxon didn't bother to answer that. Started on past them.

Staggers said, "Say, Jim."

Shit. "What is it?"

"Well, I've been thinking about making some improvements over at the roundhouse," the old man said. "Put in a few new display cases, maybe fix up those coaches for show. I could use some help if I go ahead and I thought maybe you—"

"Forget it," Maxon said. "I'm not interested."

Staggers shifted the nub of a cigar from one side of his mouth to the other. "Give it some thought before you say no, son."

"Don't have to. I don't want your charity."

"I'm not offering charity, I'm offering a part-time job. Hell, Jim, you worked on the rail crew at the mill, you know trains almost as well as you know logging. You'd be right at home working with me."

"I told you, I'm not interested."

Evans began, "I think it's a fine idea myself—"

"Then you do it, Burt," Maxon said, and abruptly stumped away from them along the road.

He could feel their eyes on him, hear the faint murmur of their voices. Talking about him behind his back, the way they always did. Poor Jim, poor cripple, won't let anybody do anything for him. Bullshit. Didn't understand him, none of them did. Wouldn't leave him alone, either. That was all he wanted, for Christ's sake, for them to leave him the hell *alone*.

When he reached his cottage he saw that Regina had left the porch light on for him again. Afraid he'd stumble in the dark, fall on his face. Like he'd done that afternoon. Light or dark, what the hell difference did it make? He threw open the gate, went up the path, up the stairs, and let himself inside. Lamp on in there too, over by the hall so he could shut it off on his way to the bedroom, wouldn't have to take any extra steps. More charity, more pity, more bullshit.

He went over there, past the lamp without turning it off, and down the hallway into the bedroom. It was dark in there, but he could make out Regina lying on her side of the bed. Only she wasn't asleep. He heard her stir, sit up as he began to undress. Watching him. Always watching him.

"Jim?"

"Yeah," he said, "go to sleep."

"I can't sleep. I've been waiting for you."

"Why? Start in about sex again, I suppose."

"No. Not unless it's what you want."

"Well, it isn't."

Maxon unbuckled his belt, dropped his pants, and stepped out of them clumsily. Went over to sit on the bed and unfasten the straps of his artificial leg. He threw the leg on the floor, and it made a clattering metallic noise as it bounced into one of the walls. Then he lay back with one arm over his eyes, not covering himself with the sheet. Sleep began to move in on him immediately.

Regina said, "Jim, I want to ask you something."

Ah, Christ. He rolled onto his side and put the pillow over his ears to shut out the sound of her voice.

Regina sat motionless in the bed, hands flat on the sheet where it covered her thighs. Jim didn't bathe much any more, or shave, or brush his teeth when he came home at night, and she could smell him lying beside her—beer and sweat, a sour lingering odor in the darkness.

"Is there anything left of our marriage?" she asked. "Is there anything worth saving?"

But she was asking the questions of herself, not him, because he had already begun to snore.

THIRTEEN

At a few minutes past midnight the state highway southwest of Springwood was almost deserted. Except for occasional logging rigs and people moving around at roadside truck stops, Hannigan and his battered Land Rover might have been alone in the warm night.

He had been driving for nearly two hours now—had returned to his cabin immediately after leaving Regina and picked up the Land Rover and taken it down out of the hills, away from Logspur. Not going anywhere, just driving. Because he had felt the need for motion, activity: sitting with his thoughts inside the empty cabin would have played hell with his nerves.

He was still not sure he had done the right thing with Regina tonight. But it had been a compulsion, too strong to fight off—a kind of necessary emotional purge. He knew now that she cared for him exactly as he had felt she did, despite her unwillingness to admit it; he had seen it reflected in her reactions and in her face, heard it in the sound of her voice, and it had given him hope and a certain relief. And yet, what if his timing had been wrong? What if he had forced her to come to terms with her feelings, her situation, prematurely? What if she wasn't ready for a new commitment and he had frightened her into reaffirming the one she already had with Jim Maxon?

He kept trying to convince himself that she would have to choose him. She had to understand as well as he did that Maxon's bitterness and self-pity were destroying him, would destroy her too if she stayed with him. But logic didn't always prevail in an emotional context—his own compulsive actions tonight were testimony to that. And there was nothing more he could do to sway her decision. He had said all there was to say, and he wouldn't, didn't dare, break his promise not to come to her again.

Now the waiting began.

Another truck stop appeared ahead. Hannigan glanced down at the gas gauge, saw that the needle had dipped toward Empty. Time to refill the tank— and time to head back home, too. He was weary of driving; by the time he got back to the cabin he might even be weary enough to sleep.

Hannigan pulled onto the apron where the pumps were, told the attendant what kind of gas he wanted. There was an all-night cafe off to one side, and he got out of the Land Rover and went over to buy a container of coffee, might help keep him alert on the return drive. The only people in the place were a couple of truck drivers sitting in a booth, and a waitress with blonde hair and gray eyes and a slender body. She reminded him of Regina. She smiled at him and he imagined Regina's smile.

She's got to choose me, he thought. If she chooses Maxon . . .

He bought his coffee, took it back out to the Land Rover. Paid the attendant and turned the jeep around and headed it back toward Logspur. He was thinking about Maxon now—a decent man who had suffered the loss of a leg and who might even be entitled to some of his sullen bitterness. And yet he realized uneasily that the sympathy he had felt for Maxon had started to fade, to be replaced by something alien to his own quiet nature.

The flip side of love.

The beginnings of hate.

FOURTEEN

It was one o'clock before Johnston finally went to bed.

He had watched two more films in his study downstairs, burned them both in the fireplace afterwards. Then, despite the fact that he was very tired, he had gone up to his office and done a little paperwork involving the mill. Too keyed up to sleep, that was the problem. Even now, as he lay in the darkness of his bedroom, he wasn't quite able to shut off his thoughts. The people in Florida and the mission on which they would embark when they received the shipment of munitions were bright images flickering across the screen of his mind—clean images, the antithesis and the scourge of what he had witnessed on the movie screen tonight.

It was hushed in the room; the only sound was the ticking of the clock-radio on the nightstand. The window to the left of the bed was open against the night's heat, and he could hear the faint whine of the big saws inside the sawmill. Soothing, but not soothing enough to make him sleep.

After a while he sighed and sat up and switched on the bedside lamp. Lighted a cigarette and smoked it down to the filter. Still wide awake, he opened the drawer in the nightstand and took out one of the packets of pornographic playing cards he kept in there, broke open the cellophane wrapping, and shuffled slowly through the cards. Men and women in groups of two, three, four. Women and women, women and ugly mechanical devices. Negroes and whites together, Orientals and whites together. Oral sex, anal sex, perverted sex: evil, evil. Fresh waves of disgust moved through him, put a sheen of perspiration on his upper lip.

When he had examined each of the cards, he threw back the bedclothes, carried the cards into the bathroom and tore them methodically into pieces and dropped the pieces into the toilet. Flushed them away. He washed his hands and face, took two aspirin, and went back to the bedroom again.

The clock-radio gave the time as 1:40.

Johnston shut off the lamp, settled down once more beneath the light top sheet. The pajamas he wore were stuffy and uncomfortable in the heat, but he would take off neither the top nor the bottom. Sleeping nude or seminude was a vulgar habit.

More time passed. He lay on his side, turned onto his stomach, turned again onto his side. His mind kept on working, but more and more sluggishly now; his discomfort faded, his muscles relaxed. Pretty soon he would sleep. Pretty soon . . .

Outside, somewhere in the compound, the Dobermans began to bark.

The sudden sounds pulled him back from the rim of unconsciousness, snapped his eyes open. He blinked, raised up on one forearm to listen. The dogs continued to set up a commotion—distantly, not anywhere near the house. Probably flushed a rabbit or a coon, Johnston thought drowsily. They did that sometimes, stopped barking after they killed it or it got away.

But he got out of bed anyway, crossed to the window. From there he could identify the direction of the noise—somewhere beyond the covered stacks of board lumber and plywood and redwood shakes near the west-side fence—but he couldn't see the fence itself or the dogs. Nothing moved anywhere within the range of his vision: motionless shadows and patches of frozen light from the pole lamps and night bulbs.

Abruptly, the barking stopped.

He stood looking out a moment longer, listening. The stillness remained unbroken; neither of the Dobermans appeared. A rabbit or a coon, all right, he thought, and pivoted and returned to the bed.

Sleep overtook him seconds after he closed his eyes.

FIFTEEN

Tully shot the first guard dog through the head, and when the second one leaped aside and flung itself at the fence, he shot it twice through the body; the silenced Colt Woodsman made little farting sounds in the darkness, inaudible more than fifty yards away. The body-shot Doberman thrashed around on the ground, legs kicking, blood coming out of its mouth. Then it stiffened, just as Tully took aim again through the wire mesh, and was as still as the other one.

Zacharias moved in on one side of Tully, Frame, holding the Thompson gun, on the other. All three of them wore thin, loose-fitting black sweaters over their Levi's and visorless black leather caps and skin-tight latex gloves. Through the fence Zacharias scanned the mill grounds, didn't see anything; the house up on the rear slope remained dark. Crickets in the underbrush around them, startled into silence by the barking of the dogs, began to set up their buzzing racket again.

Zacharias touched Tully's arm, nodded. Tully tucked his Woodsman inside his belt and got the wire cutters out of his pocket. Knelt in front of the fence to work with them down low to the ground. Frame stood flat-footed with the Thompson gun canted muzzle down along his right leg, alternately watching Tully and the empty compound. None of them said anything.

It took Tully ten minutes to open a section in the cyclone mesh—two vertical cuts three feet high and one three-foot horizontal cut across the bottom, making a square panel attached only at the top. He put the wire cutters away, then started to bend the section back and up so they could crawl through.

From upslope on the county road behind them, faintly, there came a steady sound: car engine, approaching car.

All three froze, looking past the turnaround where the double-trailer rig was parked. The engine sound grew louder. The car was still hidden from sight but there was a suggestion of bobbing light in the trees on the far side of the road. Zacharias said, "Down, get down." Tully let go of the section of fence, kicked it back into place, and the three of them dropped flat in the underbrush.

The spill of light in the trees brightened and then swung over onto the roadway as the car came through the final curve above them. Zacharias stared at the black outlines of the car, his muscles bunched with tension, looking for the dome light or whip antenna that would mean it was a sheriff's patrol. But the roof line was smooth, there was no antenna jutting up at the rear. Just a car, looked for Christ's sake like an old Hudson. It slowed as it passed the truck, but the brake lights didn't come on. It kept on going down the hill. Zacharias followed it with his eyes until it vanished behind a screen of woods near the mill gate.

Beside him Frame let out a breath, started to get up, but Zacharias put a hand on his arm and kept him down. "Give it a couple of minutes," he said in a whisper. "Make sure he doesn't come back."

They waited. And the road remained deserted. Except for the crickets and the distant whirring that came from the sawmill, the night was wrapped in silence.

Tully said finally, "It's okay, Mel. Just one of the

townspeople coming home late. Didn't pay any attention to the truck."

"Yeah," Zacharias said. He raised his head and looked back at the compound. Nothing had changed in there. "All right."

They got up and moved quickly to the fence. When Tully lifted the cut section again, Zacharias went through first on his hands and knees. Frame handed him the Thompson gun, crawled in beside him and then turned to hold the section for Tully. Pulled it back into place after him.

The three of them went past the dead dogs, Tully taking charge of the Thompson, and through the shadows to the closest of the lean-tos. Along the rows of board lumber, past a second lean-to and stacks of plywood sheets, and across to where three huge conical mounds of sawdust loomed black against the starlit sky. The smell of the sawdust was sharp in the air—too sharp, it made you want to sneeze. Zacharias began to breathe through his mouth.

They stopped behind one of the mounds, putting it between them and the lighted sawmill across the compound. Fifty yards to their left was a big squat metal tank that probably contained gasoline or diesel fuel; rail tracks ran past on the far side of it and one of the dirt roads that crisscrossed the compound paralleled the tracks on the near side. Beyond the tank was a hundred yards of ground sloping up to where the house was. There was plenty of cover between the sawdust mounds and the tank—open stacks of beam lumber and redwood blocks, a small crane and a couple of trucks parked off the dirt road—but that hundred yards of slope had nothing on it except three widely spaced trees and some low shrubs. And it was all lighted by half a dozen yellow globes mounted on top of wooden poles.

Zacharias put his mouth close to Tully's ear and said, "Open ground up there, too much light."

Tully nodded, raised an arm and pointed back and up toward the northwest, where the cyclone fence ran through a line of trees that hadn't been cleared off. Inside and outside the compound, the trees extended around behind the house. There was still thirty yards or so of open and illuminated ground between the woods and the house, on the west side and in back, but if they came in from the rear they couldn't be seen by anybody at the gate or at the sawmill.

Zacharias nodded in return, and they ran humped over away from the sawdust mounds to the fuel tank. From there he could see part of the mill gate and all of the gatehouse in the distance. Lights on inside the gatehouse but no sign of anybody down there. Or anywhere else in the area.

With the tank at their backs they ran diagonally toward the fence, keeping to the shadows thrown by more stacks of covered lumber. They had to cross forty yards of open ground near the fence, at the edge of the glow from the night lights, and when they got up into the trees Zacharias halted them to recon the compound again. But nobody had come out of the sawmill or the gatehouse, and Johnston's house was still dark and silent.

Moving single file, Zacharias in front, they went up through the trees. The closer they got to the house, the more carefully they watched where they stepped. Sounds carried on a hot night like this, Tully and Frame knew that as well as he did, and the ground was littered with small dry branches and brittle twigs.

When they reached a point opposite the rear corner, he stopped and gave the house a long look past low-hanging evergreen boughs. Two windows in the side wall on the first floor, both of them closed. Across the rear width was a veranda supported by pillars latticed with a lot of fancy wood curlicues; more curlicues hung down from the eaves. He couldn't tell if any of the windows flanking the back door were open—too many shadows.

He led them out of the trees, all three men running lightly on the balls of their feet, and across to where a set of warped-looking stairs gave access to the veranda. They hunkered down there to listen. Silence from inside the house. Zacharias leaned up to peer at the windows: shut tight, all of them. He could go up there and check each one—make sure there was no alarm system, see if one was unlocked—but he didn't want to do that unless they weren't able to find another way in. Old wood like those stairs and the veranda floor was liable to creak loud as hell when you put your weight on it.

He motioned Tully and Frame to stay where they were, pushed up into a crouch and went around to the west-side wall. At the nearest window he ran his fingers around the frame, squinted at the glass. There was a shade pulled down on the inside, and he got the pencil flash out of his pocket, shielded it with his hand, and moved the beam along the circumference of the window. No wires or photoelectric cells or metallic taping, nothing to indicate an alarm system. Satisfied, he put the flash away and got a grip on the bottom of the sash and gave it just enough upward pressure to find out whether or not it would open. It wouldn't—it was either locked or stuck tight. He moved to the second window, tugged up on its sash in the same way. And with the same results.

When he came back around the corner, Tully and Frame were both down on one knee, looking at him. Zacharias shook his head, glided past them to the east corner. Looked around it. The sawmill was visible from there, but the gate and the gatehouse were obscured by a long tin-roofed train shed. Still nobody down there moving around. He eased along the wall to the first window, tested it: locked or stuck like the others. Same thing with the next in line.

The third window, nearest the front, was open by a couple of inches.

Zacharias hooked his hands under the sash, lifted. Easily, noiselessly, it slid up a few more inches. The curtain inside billowed a little in the night breeze, but without sound. He stepped away, went back around the corner to where he could see Tully and Frame, and waved at them to come ahead.

The three of them grouped around the open window. Zacharias got another grip on the sash and eased it up slowly until it began to bind, with the opening a little better than two feet high—enough room for them to get through. The window was set low enough to the ground that Zacharias could swing a leg up and over the sill. He did that, bending his back and his head under the sash until he was sitting astraddle the sill. Lowered his right leg carefully to the floor inside, felt the soft cushion of carpeting beneath his shoe and anchored the foot on it. Then he put his weight on that foot, swung his body up inside, brought his left leg through. He did all that without making a sound.

He turned, pushed the curtain aside and stood for a moment looking over the room he was in. Seemed to

71

be a study or a den. He could make out the black shapes of a desk, a couch, a couple of chairs, bookshelves, a movie screen and a 16-millimeter projector. The door on the far side of the room was closed. He took out the pencil flash again, shielding the lens, and put it on long enough to check the floor for electrical cords or other obstructions and to determine the exact positioning of the furniture. The floor around the window was clear; the closest thing was the desk, ten feet away on the left, and the path across to the door was clear except for one of the chairs.

There was a telephone sitting on a corner of the desk. Zacharias moved over to it on his toes; the carpeting muffled his steps, and the boards beneath it didn't creak. He lifted the receiver, held it to his ear—dial tone—and then laid it down gently on the desktop, keeping the line open.

He went back to the window, beckoned to Tully's white face and Frame's black one watching from outside. Frame came in first, duplicating Zacharias' method, not making any noise either. When he was standing inside the room, Zacharias pointed at the desk and put the flash on again, just for a second, to show him the open telephone line. Frame nodded, cat-walked over, lifted the handset and stood with it pressed to his ear. Nodded again and made a circle with the thumb and forefinger of his free hand.

Tully passed the Thompson gun through to Zacharias, swung his leg up over the sill. He straddled it all right, got his head and his broad back under the sash, but when he started to raise up inside, his shoulder caught the sash's bottom edge. The window rattled—not loud, but loud enough to freeze all three in position.

They listened.

Stillness.

Zacharias waited a full minute. Then he made a fist of his left hand and put it up close to Tully's face, telling him mutely to watch what the hell he was doing. Tully obeyed, came in the rest of the way without disturbing the night hush that enveloped the house. He took the Thompson gun again.

With the flash, Zacharias briefly showed Tully the way across to the door. Tully stepped behind him and they went to it, around the chair. Zacharias rotated the knob, eased the door open a few inches and peered through the crack. Hallway, carpeted like the room they were in. He widened the opening and stepped through, Tully behind him, and padded down the hall past an open bathroom door and another hallway that right-angled to the back of the house. The hall opened up into an entrance foyer with a staircase on the far side leading up to the second floor. Beyond the staircase was a wide archway that gave into what looked to be the living room.

They moved over to the foot of the stairs. Zacharias could hear the ticking of a clock somewhere in the living room; that was the only sound. The stairs were carpeted, too, but only in the center. He looked up to the second-floor landing, could just make out two closed doors, one on either side. Johnston's bedroom figured to be up there, all right. House like this, people always had their bedrooms on the upper floor.

Cautiously, Tully at his heels, he started to climb.

SIXTEEN

Through a thin haze of sleep, Johnston heard the bed-room door open, but it wasn't until the lights went on that he came fully awake. He sat bolt upright in bed, blinking, rubbing in reflex at his eyes. There was a moment of confusion and half-blindness; then his mind cleared and his vision cleared, and he was staring across at two men he had never seen before, one of them holding a silenced handgun and the other one a submachine gun.

His first lucid thought was: Government agents, they found out about the shipment, they found out what we're planning to do.

But then he saw them more distinctly, noticed the clothes they were wearing, and when the lean one with the handgun said, "Just stay calm, Johnston, nothing's going to happen to you as long as you're calm," he knew they weren't government agents at all. Disbelief gave way to outrage; his back stiffened and his hands curled into white-knuckled fists.

"Who are you people?" he demanded. "How did you get in here? You have no right—"

"Calm, remember? Nice and cool."

The short fat one said, "Otherwise . . ." He left the sentence unfinished, moved the submachine gun to underscore his meaning.

"What do you want?" Johnston asked.

They didn't answer him. The lean one crossed the room to the nightstand at Johnston's elbow, but keep-ing a distance between them, and picked up the re-ceiver of the telephone there. He said immediately, "Okay. Upstairs, second door on your right." Which told Johnston there was a third man in the house, holding one of the downstairs extension lines open. Without waiting for a response, the lean man replaced the handset and then backed away to stand beside the fat one again.

He said then, "Get out of bed."

"Why? What for?"

"Do what you're told. Out."

Johnston hesitated, but there was no sense in resisting. He swung his legs off the bed, stood up slowly.

The lean one said, "All right. Now get dressed."

Johnston stepped sideways to the chair on which he had laid out his clothing, picked up his trousers and began to put them on over his pajama bottoms. He would not take the pajamas off in front of these men; he would not expose his body to their eyes. He got both legs into the trousers, and as he drew them up over his hips there was the sound of hurrying footsteps out in the hallway. A moment later the third man came into the bedroom.

A Negro came into the bedroom.

Johnston went rigid. A Negro, a black man—in his house, in his bedroom, looking at him while he was half-undressed. Leering at him the way the niggers in the pornographic films and still photos and playing cards leered at naked white sluts. Pointing another silenced handgun at him. Whites threatening him was repellent enough, but a black, a nigger—

He said it aloud: "A nigger. A goddamn nigger."

The black one stared at him with his lips peeling in against his teeth. A vein swelled on his forehead, his eyes flashed like an animal's. He took a step forward.

The lean one put a hand on the black's arm. "Easy," he said.

"Yeah. Easy."

Johnston said, "I won't have a nigger in my house."

"Call me a nigger one more time," the black said, "I'll tear your tongue out and stuff it up your ass. You hear that, whitey?"

"Easy, damn it," the lean one said. Then, to Johnston in a chill voice, "I'm not going to take any crap off you, mister. Get dressed!"

Johnston could feel himself trembling. The tension in the room was almost palpable, and he sensed that they would not hesitate to kill him if he provoked them. He drew a breath, got himself under control. Took his eyes off the nigger; he would not look at the nigger again; there was no nigger here any more. He turned sideways to zip up his trousers and then began to put on his shirt.

Carefully he said, "I don't keep any money in the house, if that's what you're after. Or any valuables, either."

"Is that so?" the lean one said.

"Yes, that's so."

"The hell it is," the fat one said. "You've got valuables, all right. A whole shed full of valuables—a couple of truckloads of valuables."

The munitions; they were after the *munitions!*

Understanding brought fear to him for the first time. Not for himself—he had never been afraid for his own life—fear for the cause, the Caribbean maneuver. His rage deepened, turned cold and calculating. He couldn't let them get away with it. It didn't matter who they were or how they had found out about the weapons; all that mattered was that they must not be allowed to steal the shipment.

Whole shed full of valuables.

His mind worked rapidly. They seemed to know he

had kept the munitions in the storage shed outside—
but could they know or suspect everything had been
loaded into the two boxcars last night? No, of course
not. If they had known or suspected it, they wouldn't
have bothered to come here after him, they would
have gone directly to the rail yard behind the roundhouse. The shipment *was* safe, then, because he
would never tell them about the boxcars. There was
nothing they could do to him to pry loose that infor-
mation; he would gladly die first.

But he didn't want to die. He had too much to live
for, too many things left to do; the world needed him.
There had to be a way to fight them or escape them . . .

He finished dressing, slid his bare feet into his
shoes and squatted to tie the laces. When he
straightened again, the lean one said, "Now go over to
the phone."

Johnston did that, stood waiting.

"What you're going to do," the lean one said, "is
call down to the gatehouse and tell the guard there
that a Hammond Freight Lines truck is going to come
along pretty soon and he's to let it pass through the
gate. It's a special delivery of personal goods, so you'll
take care of it yourself. You got all that?"

"Yes."

"Give it back to me."

"A Hammond Freight Lines truck is going to come
along pretty soon and the guard is to let it pass
through the gate. It's a special delivery of personal
goods, I'll take care of it myself."

"Okay. If he asks you any questions, tell him to do
what he's told, and hang up."

"He won't ask questions."

"Because he's had orders like that before, right?"

Johnston was silent. So they knew about that too, how the weapons had been trucked in in small late-night shipments over the past several months. They seemed to know everything about the munitions—almost everything. But not enough.

"You say anything else to the guard, anything at all," the lean one said, "we'll blow you away. Understood?"

"Understood."

"Make the call."

Johnston pushed the mill-line button on the telephone, lifted the receiver and dialed the two-digit number for the gatehouse. Fred Oldaker, the night guard, came on immediately. Johnston repeated the message as instructed, listened to Oldaker say, "Yes sir," and then hung up.

"Good," the lean one said. "Just fine."

Without looking at him Johnston asked, "Now what?"

"Now we go take a look at your valuables."

SEVENTEEN

They left the house through the rear door, and when they came down off the veranda stairs Zacharias stopped them and said to Tully, "Go ahead and pick up the truck. We'll handle it here."

"Right."

Tully turned the Thompson gun over to Frame, hurried away toward the trees to the west. Zacharias would rather have sent Frame for the truck because Frame handled the big rig better than Tully did. But Tully knew the layout of the compound, and he was white. Big black dude like Frame came driving up in the truck at this hour of night, the guy on the gate might get a little nervous and start wondering. They couldn't afford to chance that, not when they had hours of work ahead of them before they were ready to leave.

When Tully reached the woods, Zacharias looked back at Johnston. Saw that he was still standing stiffly, arms flat against his sides, staring straight ahead. Johnston had pretty much stopped looking at any of them up in the bedroom, seemed to be making a particular point of not looking at Frame. He wasn't giving them any mouth-hassle, either. But he was crazy as hell—the way he'd started in on Frame confirmed that—and there was no way of telling what might be running around inside his head. As soon as they were ready to load the trailers, they'd have to put his lights out for good. Let Frame do it, maybe. Verne was still pissed about the old bastard calling him a nigger; you could see it in the way he was glaring now at the back of Johnston's head. He'd want to pull the trigger, all right.

"Okay," Zacharias said. "Move out."

Johnston said, "Where?"

"You know where. Move."

He moved. Did a kind of military right face and headed for the east corner of the house. Zacharias and Frame followed by a couple of steps, flanking him, Frame holding the Thompson gun in close to his body. They went around the corner and along the side wall. Zacharias scanned the compound left to right, right to left, but there was still nothing to see except light and shadow and emptiness.

The shed—a tin-roofed job with plank walls, built lower to the ground than a barn and about half the size—was a hundred yards away, set at an angle between the house and a couple of big kilns. One of the mill roads let up in front of the shed, and a rail spur looped around to parallel the south wall, ending at a right angle to the road. In the near wall, facing west, were what looked like eight-foot-high double doors. There weren't any windows that Zacharias could see.

Johnston started straight down across the open lighted ground, but Zacharias stepped up to him quickly and punched his arm and said, "Off to the left; keep the shed in front of us."

He didn't get any argument; Johnston changed direction immediately, led them due east and then across the road above where the shed was. They went down to it, into the shadows along the west wall. When they came up to the double doors, Zacharias saw that they were fastened in the center by a padlock drawn through iron hasps on each half. They would open outward and swing back against the wall, and the truck could be backed off the road and right up to them for easy loading.

Without being told, Johnston got a ring of keys out of his pants pocket, picked one out and opened the padlock. Left it hanging from one of the hasps and started to pull the doors open.

"I'll do it," Zacharias said. "You just back up out of the way."

Johnston let go of the door handles, retreated half a dozen paces. Zacharias moved away from Frame and took the handles himself and tugged the doors open. The hinges squeaked a little as the two halves fanned out on either side of him, but that kind of noise meant nothing now. He looked inside, couldn't make out much of anything in the blackness, and turned to look at Johnston.

"How do you put the lights on?"

"Switches on the wall inside, to your left."

Moving forward again, into the hot stuffy interior of the shed, Zacharias felt around on the wall until he found the bank of switches. He flipped one of them. A screened globe attached to one of the roof beams near the center rear came on, letting him see most of the shed's floor space.

It was empty.

The whole damned building was *empty*.

Surprise and sudden fury blended together inside Zacharias. He heard Frame say, "What the fuck?" behind him, started to pivot around again, out of the doorway.

And that was when Johnston made his break.

One of the door halves suddenly came flying inward, slapped against the muzzle of the Thompson gun and knocked the gun and Frame in toward Zacharias: Frame had been standing too close to the goddamn door and must have taken his eyes off Johnston for a second—just long enough for Johnston to grab the door edge and swing it forward. Frame made a startled noise, staggered a step and almost ran into Zacharias before he caught his balance. Zacharias shoved past him savagely and kicked the door half out of the way, dragging his Woodsman up, looking for Johnston.

Saw him twenty yards away, running in close to the shed wall.

Frame lunged forward. Zacharias fired past him at Johnston's legs—not wanting to kill him yet; they didn't know what had happened to the ordnance—but it was a hurried shot and the bullet gouged splinters out of the wall a foot wide of the mark. He steadied his arm, fired low again. Missed again because Johnston had reached the corner, ducked around it.

Frame was already running, carrying the Thompson gun up in front of his body as if he was thinking about using it. Grimacing, Zacharias pounded up beside him and knocked the muzzle down with his left forearm. They were near the corner by then and he could see Johnston on the far side of the rail spur, thirty yards distant and heading south, away from the kilns, toward the road down there that ran alongside the beam lumber and the redwood blocks and straight to the sawmill. He wanted to squeeze off a third round, didn't do it—you couldn't hit anybody with a silenced .22 while you were on the run, and now that they were coming out into the open there was the chance somebody might see the muzzle flash.

Zacharias snapped at Frame, "Cut him off, cut him off!" and veered off at a sharp angle to his left.

Just before Johnston got to the road, he threw a look over his shoulder, saw the two of them coming and seemed to understand right away that he couldn't get to the sawmill before they got to him. Zacharias thought Johnston was going to start yelling, knew if that happened he'd have to shut him up immediately. Use the Thompson if it came down to that, and then get the hell out of here, screw the ordnance.

But Johnston didn't start yelling. And he didn't keep on going toward the sawmill. Instead he cut back to the west, across the road, plunged around one of the stacks of beam lumber, and vanished.

Zacharias looked over toward the sawmill as he ran, didn't see a sign of anybody, and put his gaze back on the beam lumber. When he and Frame reached the road, they pulled up on the west side of it, in the shadows, and stood listening. From the west there came faint scuffling sounds, then the sounds stopped and the night was quiet except for the rasp of their breathing.

He leaned close to Frame and said between clamped teeth, "Get in there after him. I'll go around this end, make sure he doesn't double back. Don't kill him unless you have to."

"Yeah," Frame said.

"He gets away, I'll have your black ass."

Frame glared at him for an instant. Then he muttered something and slid forward between two of the lumber stacks and was gone.

Zacharias went the other way, around to the ten yards of open space separating the beam lumber from the redwood blocks. The stacks were a good thirty yards wide and maybe seventy-five yards long, with narrow walkways between rows. Beyond were more open ground and the conical mounds of sawdust they had passed on their way in. Johnston wasn't going to be able to come back this way, not without Zacharias seeing him. He had boxed himself into this part of the compound.

Slowly, moving in a noiseless crouch, Zacharias began to make his way forward.

EIGHTEEN

Johnston came out of the lumber to the west, paused there with his back up against the blunt end of a beam. He could hear at least one of the hijackers moving around somewhere behind him, not too close, not yet. Pulse hammered in his ears, and his face and hands were damp with sweat; but he wasn't afraid. Even now he was not the slightest bit afraid. What he felt instead was a kind of exhilaration—a desperate excitement.

Running, he had thought of shouting for help but had discarded the idea immediately. They might have used the submachine gun on him if he had done that—and what could his men do, anyhow, against three armed and dangerous thieves? No, it was him against them. Him alone. He had gotten away from them at the shed and he would get away from them now, too. Save himself and insure the safety of the munitions and the secrecy of his allegiance to the cause. Outwit them as he would one day outwit the enemies of democracy.

There was a flatbed truck parked a few rods away, just off the road, and Johnston let his eyes linger on it. Had the last man who'd used it left the keys inside? With the flatbed he could get clear of the two hijackers, reach the gate in time to prevent the fat one from bringing their truck inside the compound. He turned sideways, bent forward at the waist, and ran quickly and silently to the flatbed. Neither the lean one nor the nigger was out on the road; both of them had gone into the lumber, both of them were still searching for him in there. He went around the rear of the flatbed, crept forward again to the driver's door. Pulled the handle down and eased the door open and leaned in across the seat to feel for the ignition.

Damn. It was empty.

Johnston withdrew, pushed the door closed but didn't relatch it. The road was still deserted. He listened, heard one of them moving around in the lumber, coming closer now to the end of the rows of beams. He swung around, putting his back to the door, and scanned the area to the west. He could make for the lean-tos to the south, or he could go up to the fuel storage tank to the north and then sprint for the trees along the fence above. Yes—the trees. If he could get into their shelter, he could either climb the fence out of the compound or, better yet, he could make it back inside the house, arm himself with the .45 automatic he kept in his study.

He shoved away from the door, moved back to the rear of the truck. Noticed as he did so that there were several three-foot-long wooden stakes lying on the open bed. On impulse he picked one of them up in his right hand, felt the solid weight of it, and held it down along his side. It was not much of a weapon against their guns, but it was something substantial to hang on to nonetheless. It gave him a sense of raw power, added to his feeling of exhilaration and invincibility.

He took another look behind him, over at the lumber. And made his run for the fuel tank on the far side of the road.

NINETEEN

When Frame couldn't find Johnston anywhere in the lumber, he finally cut around one of the rows and went back out toward the road. And there the son of a bitch was, running toward that big tank across the way.

Frame stepped back into the shadows and watched Johnston get to the tank, duck out of sight behind it. No time to bring Zacharias into it. By the time he found Mel, Johnston would get away—maybe get clear out of the compound. Hell with Zacharias anyway, him and his tough talk and his jive-ass racial cracks and his sweet little strike that couldn't miss. That crazy honky bigot up there was all his; he'd fix that mother good and plenty.

He ran on the balls of his feet, away from the lumber, straight across the road, and came in on the tank to the west. There was no sign of Johnston in the darkness on that side or on the open ground beyond; he was either directly behind the tank or over on the east side. Without slowing, Frame turned his body sideways as he neared the tank, sprinted along it and five feet away from it.

He heard Johnston before he saw him—and Johnston heard Frame. There were shuffling noises on the rear side of the tank, the faint metallic sound of something glancing against the tank's casing. Then Frame barreled out into the open, and in the blackness Johnston appeared, just starting to run, looking back over his shoulder. But less than fifteen yards separated them, and when Frame veered toward him and snapped, "Hold it! I'll cut you in half, man," Johnston pulled up and whirled around to face him.

With fifteen feet between them, Frame hauled up, too. Johnston had a piece of wood in one hand, and he raised it over his head and began to back away. Frame let him do it, because he was backing up toward the tank. When Johnston's back butted up against the casing he spread his feet and pointed a finger at Frame as if he were aiming a gun. He still held the piece of wood upraised in his other hand.

"Get away from me, nigger," he said.

Frame could feel his stomach knotting up with hatred. He moved a couple of steps closer, sliding his finger back and forth across the trigger of the Thompson gun. "Where's that ordnance? What'd you do with it?"

Johnston seemed to smile. His eyes were wide, gleaming palely in the darkness. Crazy. Crazy as hell. "It's gone," he said. "Shipped out last night."

"Shipped out where?"

"Where you'll never find it."

That tore it; that tore it just fine. The whole thing was blown; a quarter-million-dollar split, the biggest strike of his life, and he was going to come out of it with nothing. And all because of this crazy honky standing in front of him.

"Did you hear me, nigger?" Johnston asked. "The munitions are gone; they're safe; you'll never get them."

The hatred was like a fire inside Frame. Nigger. That's all he'd been hearing all day, first from Zacharias and then from Johnston. You're a city boy, boy. Fix you up with another white woman. How about some ribs and watermelon? Big black buck like you. I'll have your black ass. You're all right for a nigger. A goddamn nigger. Get away from me, nigger. Nigger, nigger, nigger.

Well, fuck Zacharias; fuck everything except doing it to Johnston and getting clear of here. Doing it to him good. He'd get that much out of it anyway.

"Keep on calling me nigger," he said softly.

"Nigger. Filthy nigger."

"Yeah. That's it. Say it again."

"Nigger. Black devil!"

"One more time, baby."

"You can't hurt me!" Johnston shouted. "There's not a nigger on earth who can hurt me!" And he started forward waving the piece of wood.

Frame squeezed the Thompson's trigger. Not thinking about the fuel storage tank behind Johnston, not thinking about anything except doing it to him, just one short burst, he heard the gun begin to chatter and saw Johnston driven backward—

Those were the last things he thought and saw and heard, the very last things, because it was the very last moment of his life.

In the second that followed, the fuel tank and all Frame's world erupted in a great mushrooming explosion of heat and sound and flame.

TWENTY

The blast knocked Zacharias off his feet and rolled him over half a dozen times on the dusty bed of the road.

He had just come out from the lumber, after hearing a voice shouting up by the tank. Then had come the hammering of the Thompson gun, and he'd had just enough time to think: Frame, you stupid—when the tank exploded. The next thing he knew he was picking himself up, dazed and bruised, and all around him was roaring fire and heat. The tank belched tongues of flame and huge clouds of black smoke, turning the night sky as bright as noon. Sparks and tracers of fire fell everywhere, dry grass was burning everywhere; tree boughs had started to blaze by the west fence; the sawdust mounds were yellow-orange pyres; the beam lumber and the redwood blocks, strewn together like the rubble of collapsed houses, were just beginning to burn.

Zacharias staggered backward, one hand up to shield his face against the waves of superheated air. It seared his skin, had already singed off his eyebrows and sideburns and part of his hair. The stench of incinerated hair and smoldering cloth made him gag. He was aware of stinging pain on his arms and legs, on his chest, and when he looked down at himself he saw that cinders had opened widening holes in his clothing. He slapped at the holes, realizing as he did that he'd managed somehow to hang onto the silenced Woodsman. Instinctively he shoved the gun inside the waistband of his pants, under the overhang of his sweater.

Behind him, over the crackling noise of the fire, he could hear men shouting in confusion and alarm—the night crew at the sawmill. He swung his head frantically from side to side, still backing away. Patches of fire everywhere he looked, rushing together in spots to build flaming barriers. No way to get out of the compound now except through the front gate.

He spun around and began to run.

TWENTY-ONE

Hannigan had just gotten back to Logspur, was just turning the Land Rover onto Highway 4 beyond the mill, when the night silence detonated with such force that the windows rattled.

The surprise as much as the noise itself nearly made him lose control of the Land Rover. He jammed on the brakes, slewed to a stop off on the verge of the road. Swung out and stood staring in disbelief at the flame and smoke geysering skyward from the mill.

Oh my God!

He raced back down the road, cut across toward the wide-open mill gate. Shouting men from the sawmill were beginning to stream toward it inside. Parked just outside the gate was the big truck-and-double-trailer rig Hannigan had passed moments ago on his way in; it had just been turning onto the mill's access road from the intersection. A short round man dressed in dark clothing was standing in front of the truck, looking over at the flames with a kind of slack-jawed fixity, as if he had been momentarily hypnotized by the sight. His face was pale under his black leather cap, glistening with sweat, and the reflected firelight made his eyes seem huge and glassy, like those of the deer heads inside The Tavern.

Hannigan went past the man, dodged through the outpouring of mill workers to the gatehouse inside. From there he could tell that the main source of the blaze was the fuel storage tank across the compound. And he could see that the entire west side was rapidly becoming sheeted with flame. Fire raced through the trees around Henry Johnston's house, had already torched one of the sheds farther east, was beginning to jacket the kilns and make them glow a hellish cherry red.

The last of the men ran toward him and he recognized Jack Bennett, the foreman of the night crew. Hannigan shouted, "Jack, what *happened*?"

Bennett slowed. "Don't know. The tank just blew."

"Was anybody over there?"

"I don't think so. We were all inside the—"

The rest of the sentence was lost in the sound of another explosion, much smaller than the eruption of the fuel tank, muffled somewhat by the thrumming of the fire. A wave of flame and gray-black smoke boiled upward a few hundred yards across the compound.

"One of the trucks!" Bennett shouted. "Jesus, we've got to get out of here; we don't have much time!"

Hannigan understood that Bennett did not just mean getting out of the mill compound: he also meant getting out of Logspur, out of the valley. And the rest of the night crew, all the village residents, would come to that same conclusion within minutes. As dry as everything around here was and as fast as that fire was spreading, this entire area would soon become an inferno.

Bennett was already rushing ahead to the gate. Hannigan started to follow, held up abruptly when something over by the tin-roofed train shed fifty yards distant caught his attention. He wheeled around, squinting—and saw it was a man running in awkward strides, outlined blackly against the high shimmering glare.

Hannigan ran over there to intercept him, help him, thinking that it must be Johnston. The air was furnace-hot now, and the billowing smoke began to clog his sinuses, making it difficult for him to breathe. He held one arm crooked in front of his eyes to protect them. When he was twenty yards from the running man he saw that it wasn't Johnston after all, that it was a lean stranger dressed in the same dark clothing as the truck driver outside. Cinders smoldered on his clothing in half a dozen places and most of his hair had been singed off. He was gasping, choking on smoke; tear streams made glistening patterns on cheeks flushed brick-red by the heat.

He didn't seem to see Hannigan, nearly collided with him. Hannigan side-stepped, got a grip on the man's arm to steady him; he could smell the sickening pungent odor of scorched hair and cloth and flesh. For a moment the stranger fought him in a half-panicked way, trying to pull free—but when Hannigan said urgently, "It's all right, I'll help you out," the man blinked, focused on him, and stopped struggling. Together, they plunged ahead for the gate.

The stranger stumbled twice, but Hannigan still had hold of his arm and kept him from falling. They skirted the gatehouse, went through the gate and past the double-trailer rig. And down the access road in the wake of the other running men.

Behind them, inside the compound, the fire hurled bulletlike bits of flaming wood at the sawmill walls and set them ablaze.

TWENTY-TWO

The explosion wrenched Maxon up out of sleep and into a half-sitting, half-crouching position on the damp bedsheet. His heart raced wildly, his head throbbed with hangover and the heaving return to consciousness. He shook himself—shaking off disorientation—and listened. Quiet again. But too quiet, as if there were more sounds which he was unable to hear yet.

Outside the southwest window, the sky was tinged with a suggestion of flickering reddish light.

Regina said in a frightened voice beside him, "My God, what was that? It sounded like—"

"An explosion, yeah."

"Jim—the mill?"

"Don't ask me. Go outside and look."

She swung out of bed immediately, caught up her robe, and pulled it over her shoulders as she ran out of the bedroom. Maxon pressed his hands to his temples, dragged them down over his beard-stubbled cheeks. Grimaced at the sour aftertaste of the beer he had drunk and stared at the faint shimmery light beyond the window. Fire?

Jesus, *fire?*

He was fully awake then. He twisted around on the bed, reached out to the bedside lamp and snapped it on. Blinking, he looked for the artificial leg, saw it lying against one wall, where he had thrown it earlier. He got off the bed, hearing doors slam in the neighboring houses now, the muted babble of voices raised in querulous alarm. He hopped over to where the prosthetic limb lay, managed to brace himself and bend down to pick it up. Hopped back to the bed again and sat on the edge and began hurriedly strapping the thing in place.

He got the harness buckled just as the screen door banged out front. A moment later Regina came running back into the bedroom. Her face was pale, her eyes even wider than usual and dark with fear.

She said, "It *is* the mill, Jim—it's on fire!"

"What's on fire?"

"The whole mill!"

"Throw me my pants and shirt. Hurry up!"

She ran to where the pile of clothing lay in the middle of the floor, picked it up and tossed it to him. He pulled his pants on, the shirt over his head. Pushed himself upright and slid his left foot into his suede loafer. Regina had stripped off her robe and nightgown, was bent over naked fumbling with her shorts. Maxon hobbled past her, out of the bedroom and along the hall and through the screen door.

When he clumped off the porch steps, onto the garden path, he came to a sharp standstill and stood staring toward the mill. A pall of twisting black smoke obliterated most of the sky in that direction; below it, where the mill buildings stood, firelight stained the night a ruddy orange color. The whole damned mill was burning, all right—but that wasn't all. The evergreens on the northwestern slope were flaming, too, the blaze feeding on the dry needles and the pitch-heavy wood.

Jesus God, he thought in awe, it's going to wipe out the town, the valley, everything.

Then he thought: The roads over there—the roads!

Maxon ran limpingly to the gate, pulled it open. Spruce Road was coming alive with cars and pickup trucks, with other townspeople running alone and in family groups. Some of the vehicles stopped to pick up those on foot; others, already full, went around them and kept on going. Everyone knew there was no time to gather personal belongings, no time to do anything except to get out of the valley before the fire blocked off the two county highways and trapped them there. Urgency and fear were as palpable in the air as the sharp wind-carried smell of smoke.

The screen door banged again behind Maxon as he stepped out to the edge of the road. He glanced back, saw Regina rush along the path wearing the shorts and a pullover blouse, and waited until she came up beside him. Then he moved onto the road, hailed the next set of headlights in the string. The lights swung toward him immediately, slid past him as the car—Joe Linscott's battered Ranchero, young Linscott and his wife sitting grim-faced inside—braked to a stop. He prodded Regina quickly around to the rear, dragged the tailgate down and levered himself up onto the bed on his buttocks. She followed suit, caught onto his arm and leaned against him as Linscott pulled away again.

Regina said something to him but he couldn't hear over the loud throbbing roar of engines. Wasn't paying attention to her anyway, because he was sliding around on his left hip to look northward over the low side wall. The fire was spreading with incredible speed, aided by gusts of the thin night breeze. Firebrands leaped from treetop to treetop on the slope above the mill, igniting millions of pine and spruce needles in bursts of roiling flame. Fountains of sparks fanned up and out against the backdrop of smoke, showered down like a grotesque fireworks display.

And as he watched it, there was no bitterness in him, no feeling of emptiness or apathy. For the first time since the accident he was facing a tragedy far greater than the loss of his leg, and the impact of it was having a profound effect on him.

It was making him care again.

TWENTY-THREE

Beside the double-trailer rig, Tully stood staring at the fire raging wildly across the compound. Part of his mind was aware of where he was and of what he was seeing and hearing—men running past him, shouts, the clouds of smoke and the moaning whisper of the flames—but another part of his mind had turned inward, opened his memory so that he was also staring with a kind of detached horror at that other fire long ago, seeing it through eleven-year-old eyes and hearing again the dying screams of his father.

His father. Big man, quick-tempered, drank too much and whored around, but still his father, still the man his mother loved. Running out of the burning house that last night with the fire eating away at his pajamas and his flesh, beating madly at the flames. And his mother shrieking, himself crying, helpless, watching his father run on fire and then fall into the street and writhe around on it, screaming, "Help me, help me!" Rushing over there with his mother to try to put him out, try to put his father *out* like a burning match. Too late. Looking at him charred and dead there in the street and hearing his mother say, "Don't look, Roy, don't look," and then having his head pulled around and held tight against her breasts.

He'd been terrified that night and he was terrified now.

Someone came up close beside him. "Come on," a voice said, "get away from here, for God's sake!"

Tully just stood there.

"Come on, mister! What's the matter with you?"

He couldn't move, couldn't speak. The flames held him transfixed.

Hands gripped his arms; he felt himself being turned away from the truck and propelled down the road. He didn't struggle, but his head snapped around because the fire was a magnetic force his eyes could not resist. He watched it all the way down the road and across the intersection and onto the grassy flat beyond.

The hands released him there and the man who had helped him kept on running into the village. But Tully stood again as he had by the truck: rigid, staring. Dimly he heard more shouting, the rumble of car engines. Saw, at the rim of his vision, two more men run out of the mill gate and come toward him on the road.

Inside his head his father screamed and screamed.

When the last two men reached him, slowed to a stop, he realized that one of them was Zacharias—and realized, too, that most of Zacharias' hair had been burned off, that his face looked burned and there were scorched holes in his clothing. Fire had almost got him, almost done to him what it had done to Tully's father. The understanding broke some of the flames' hypnotic hold on his mind, made him blink and focus more clearly on Zacharias.

The other man, a big redhead, looked at Tully. And then looked at Zacharias and said, "You going to be okay?"

"Yeah."

"What about you?" the man asked Tully. "You all right?"

Panic was beginning to work inside him now. Words came out of his throat in a thick rush: "I'm not going to die the way he did."

"The way who did?"

"All in flames," Tully said. "Screaming." He swung around, looked into the village. Headlights coming on the streets, cars and pickup trucks streaming this way. "Got to get out of here, got to get away from that fire!"

Zacharias said, "Christ, what's the matter with—"

But Tully was already running for the intersection.

TWENTY-FOUR

Hannigan took out after the short round man, the other stranger beside him. The entire mill was blazing now, and the fire had overrun its eastern boundaries; the high timberland to the northwest, north, and northeast was coated with leaping flames that cast weird shifting patterns across the sky. Smoke partially obliterated Highway 19 and was beginning to undulate across Highway 4 as well.

Any second now fire's going to jump both those roads.

The thought put ripples of cold on Hannigan's back. He swiveled his gaze to the village, saw the cars pouring along Main Street, lined out like a caravan. More vehicles moved onto Mill Street to the east, in front of the roundhouse. All the buildings had a glazed look in the flickering reddish light: surreal, monstrous.

The first set of headlights came through the Main Street loop just as the short round man got to the intersection. He waved his arms frenziedly over his head, jumped out in front of the car. It cut sharply to the left to avoid him and skidded to a stop.

Hannigan looked over at Highway 19 again—and a firebrand hurtled out of the blaze on the northwest side and across the road. One of the trees there flashed with sudden fire as all its dry surfaces ignited simultaneously; twigs and branches were flung straight up into the air and consumed before they could fall. A moment later that tree became a black, smoldering skeleton while the fire raced on to the ones surrounding it.

By the time Hannigan got to where the short round man was clawing at the door handle on the car, the road ahead was shrouded in smoke and walled on both sides by crackling flames.

And when he swung around to look at Highway 4 he saw the same thing happening up there.

The lead cars on Mill Street ground to a halt when their drivers, too, saw the barrier of smoke and fire ahead of them. Behind them, and behind the pack leader on Main Street, the drivers who couldn't see the roads clearly began honking their horns, and there were several seconds of chaotic jockeying for position. Then everyone seemed to realize at once why the caravans had quit moving. All of the headlights became stationary, and men and women and children spilled out of the vehicles, running. The moaning thunder of the fire was punctuated with shouts and shrill, frightened cries.

Grunting, the short round man finally dragged the car door open, tried to fling himself inside. But the other people in there were already pushing their way out through the driver's door, through both rear doors. Hannigan got a grip on the back of the stranger's sweater, heaved him backward, and wrapped his long muscled arms around him. The round man struggled frantically, soundlessly, and the lunging impetus of his body made Hannigan stagger. But he tightened his hold, managed to get his legs planted wide apart and the straining man braced in place against his left knee.

The other stranger came into it then. Caught the front of the round one's sweater with his left hand and slapped him sharply across the face with the flattened palm of his right. "Snap out of it, Roy, goddamn it! Snap out of it!"

Roy, the round man, stopped struggling; his muscles stiffened, then relaxed. He was breathing very fast through his nose and mouth, but still not making any other sound. When Hannigan eased the pressure of his hold, Roy didn't try to pull away again. Hannigan let him go, stepped back. The round man just stood there, looking up at the fire, not moving at all. He seemed to have reverted to a kind of catatonic shock. Hannigan had seen that sort of fluxing reaction in a person before; it always meant a phobia of some kind—a morbid fear of fire, in Roy's case. The man was a pyrophobe, all right.

The lean stranger had a grip on the round one's arm now, watching him. Hannigan pivoted, saw people swarming around, some of them out in the middle of the intersection. Some of the children were whimpering and coughing; a few of the very young ones were crying loudly. The faces of the men and women had an unnatural look in the dancing firelight—twisted and shapeless with fear, like mummers' masks stained red-orange and sooty black.

Regina, he thought.

He looked for her, located her standing beside Jim Maxon, one hand clutching Maxon's arm as though for support. Impulsively he started toward her. And then checked himself. There was nothing he could do for her now, nothing he could say to her.

A feeling of desperate helplessness came over him. He wheeled around again to face the fire. Masses of flame swept like live things across the tops of the trees from northwest to northeast, and less than three hundred yards upslope both county roads were completely invisible beneath dense coagulations of smoke. Growing wider by the second, the blaze was already spread out before them like a gigantic wall a thousand yards long.

Wildfire.

And both roads to safety impassably blocked.

We're trapped, he thought. God help us, we're trapped.

PART TWO: HOLOCAUST

TWENTY-FIVE

Any second now there was going to be mass panic.

Ed Staggers could see it in the faces of the people around him, hear it in the cries of the children and in the shrill voices of the men and women. *Trapped, we're trapped!* It was building, spreading with the same destructive speed of the fire; it clogged the air as thickly as the scorching fire-wind and the choking gray smoke.

We're trapped! There's no way out!

He battled the thrust of it inside himself, tightened his arm around his wife's narrow shoulders. He couldn't seem to think clearly. None of them was thinking clearly. They were all losing their individuality, being transformed by the force of combined terror into an unreasoning mob.

No way out!

Except that there is, he thought suddenly.

The Baldwin locomotive inside the roundhouse, the coach cars over on the siding, the rail tracks to Springwood.

By rail, by rail!

The realization was like a sharp mental slap: it broke the panic's hold on him, restored his ability to function. He could feel his face swelling with urgency, the need to take command before it was too late. He stepped quickly away from his wife, cupped his hands to his mouth to make himself heard over the sound of the fire.

"Listen, all of you!" he bellowed. "Listen to me! We've still got a chance! Hitch up the locomotive to the coaches—we can get out by train!"

For a moment it seemed that none of them comprehended what he was saying; the milling confusion, the mounting panic went on unchecked. Then, when he shouted it again—"We can get out by train!"—the sense of the words got through to them. Heads and bodies turned in his direction, there was a sudden rising babble of voices. The panic shattered like glass and the shards were swept away by a surge of desperate hope. People began running toward him, converging on him.

"He's right!" Al Logan yelled. "We can still make it."

"The roundhouse!" Fred Oldaker shouted. "Get to the roundhouse—"

In that instant, over by the mill gate, there was another rocketing explosion.

Staggers saw flame and smoke balloon upward, felt the blast of fiery wind, and knew without thinking about it that it was the big double-trailer rig he had seen parked before the gate. Sparks and bits of molten metal hailed down in all directions, peppered the area where they were, clattered off the surfaces of the parked cars and pickups. Patches of dry grass began to burn immediately in half a dozen different places.

The explosion galvanized them into action, all of them at once like a herd of animals stampeding—only now with a unified direction and purpose. Men and women scooped up the younger children, and with

Staggers leading them, they ran at an angle across the village green toward the roundhouse looming against the smoke-hazed sky.

Coughing, panting for breath, Staggers looked off to the northeast as he cleared the last of the oak trees in the park. The fire raged along the ridge there, around and behind the rail yard. Blocks of flame streaked through treetops, fragmented and erupted forward like mortar shells that landed fifty, a hundred yards ahead of the main blaze, and exploded everything they touched. But there were better than three hundred yards of open ground between the fire's perimeter and the siding where the coaches waited, nearly all of it hard-packed earth that was grassless and treeless, crisscrossed by rail spurs and sidings. Nothing much there for the blaze to feed on—unless one of those mortarlike firebrands hurtled out and hit the wooden side paneling on either of the coaches.

But there was a much greater and more immediate danger than that: smoke inhalation and the savage heat. None of them would be able to withstand either of those for long. If they didn't get clear of the village in a damned fast time, people were going to start dropping left and right . . .

Staggers cut between two of the string of vehicles on Mill Street, pulled up in the visitors' parking lot fronting the roundhouse. Spun around as the others streamed in after him. He fought his breathing under control, began barking out the names of men who had worked on the rail crew at the mill and acted as yardmen and train crew on the annual run to the county fair in July.

"Linscott, Baker, Tyrell, Adcock! Come with me! The rest of you head south, out into the yards—spread out along the tracks; we'll pick you up there!"

No one questioned the orders. They had all accepted his authority, tacitly placed the responsibility for their safety in his hands. But Staggers didn't let himself think about the burden of that. He turned for the roundhouse door, the four men he had named grouping with him, while the rest of the villagers turned away in a body and rushed off into the yard.

Staggers got the door open, plunged inside and hit the light switches. "Open the engine doors," he shouted to Adcock. And to Tyrell, "Man the turntable." And to Linscott, "Joe, you and Bake get the water hose up into the boiler tank."

The five of them ran across the whitewashed floor, fanning out. Staggers went straight to the Baldwin locomotive, swung up inside the cab. Plenty of coal in the tender, more than enough to get them the fifteen miles to Springwood; he always ordered in a fresh supply after the trip to the county fair. He leaned down to open one of the tankboxes, pulled out an oilcan. Which of the others for fireman? he was thinking. Ben Kiley had always handled the job in the past, but Kiley wasn't here—he didn't live in Logspur, was one of the few employees who commuted to the mill from Springwood. Linscott, then? Linscott was a good man, despite his youth, but he had never worked on a steam locomotive. None of them had worked on a steam locomotive. Except—

And a voice said abruptly from alongside the cab below, as if tuned into and responding to his thoughts, "You're going to need a fireman, Ed. I'm your man."

Staggers straightened up, looked around.

The voice belonged to Jim Maxon.

TWENTY-SIX

Maxon caught the handbar on the side of the cab, got his left foot anchored on the running board, and launched himself up through the gangway to the deck inside. He limped past Staggers to the tender, grabbed the shovel that hung from its bulkhead. Half-turned then to face the old man.

"There's no time to argue, Ed," he said grimly. "I'm the only one with experience at the job. And I can handle it, don't worry. I'm going to handle it."

Staggers' seamed face was expressionless. His eyes bored into Maxon's for three or four seconds, then he nodded once, said, "All right, son, load her up," and turned immediately and climbed down out of the cab to oil up.

Maxon was relieved and a little surprised. He'd expected an argument, to have to fight to join Staggers here in the cab. The need to take the fireman's job had come over him when he'd stumped up outside the roundhouse—Regina on one side of him and Joe Linscott on the other, helping him run—and Staggers began shouting out his orders. The lives of eighty people were at stake, people who'd once been his friends—that was part of it. But there was more to it than that. He wanted to take the fireman's job, *had* to take it, because it was something he was qualified for, even with one leg: he'd worked the firebox on the old steam switch engine those summers with his father in Eureka. And it meant being useful again instead of useless. His home, his town were going to be wiped out; a chance to be whole again for a few short hours was all he had left.

He swung the shovel into the tender, scooped up coal, pivoted on his good leg and drove his aluminum foot against the pedal on the floor in front of the firebox. The butterfly doors slapped open. He scattered coal over the grate inside, turned back to the tender and began to repeat the process. The artificial leg wasn't any problem now, but he'd have to be damned careful to watch his balance once they were in motion. And he would, all right. No way was he going to let the leg keep him from seeing this through. No way.

Through the side glass and the narrow, oblong front glass panels he could see the others working as he shoveled. Linscott and Baker had dragged the heavy water hose across the floor and up into the boiler tank and Baker had turned the spigot on; the water gushing into the tank made a hissing metallic sound. Tyrell had started the electric motor that operated the turntable, used the pushbar to line up the track, locked it down, and was running out now through the open engine doors to join Adcock on the yard switches.

Maxon could also see, now the doors were open, that the entire eastern slope beyond the yard was ablaze. Columns of smoke danced above the heaving span of flames, altering direction high up in the thin gusts and drafts of wind. The heat burned in his lungs again, and he tightened his jaws to keep himself from coughing.

Fleetingly he thought of Regina, wondered if she was all right. She'd tried to stop him when he started for the roundhouse, but he had pushed her away roughly, yelled to her to go with the others. That bastard Hannigan had taken her arm and pulled her along toward the yard. She would never stop thinking of him as a helpless cripple, would never stop believing he had to be watched over and protected. Well, for a little while he was going to be the one to do the protecting. He didn't have to worry about her; she'd be okay. All of them would be okay. He and Staggers would see to that.

The firebox was half full when the old man came up beside him again. Staggers fired up the boiler, put on the lamp that hung from the walnut paneling on the front bulkhead, and began turning valve handles and opening cylinder cocks and checking the manifold gauges. When the water glass told him the tank was full, he leaned out of the side window to shout at Baker, "Okay, shut her down!"

Baker closed the spigot, and Linscott dragged the hose free of the tank and threw it down out of the way. Then the two of them sprinted out into the yard.

Maxon watched the steam gauge, high on the boiler butt. The needle climbed slowly. The glow inside the firebox flared a hotter and brighter red each time he pedaled open the butterfly doors, and the cab filled with an increasing volume of noise—the blast of the firebox, the stuttering clamor of valves, the staccato beat of the exhaust.

He called across to Staggers, "We're about ready, Ed."

"Pretty quick. Keep stoking."

Another twenty seconds went by. Then Staggers took his eyes off the steam gauge, called, "Okay!" to Maxon, flipped the headlight on, released the brakes, and wrapped his left hand around the throttle. Gave her some steam to get them moving. The drivers clanked and began to turn, and the locomotive jolted forward, hissing steam, its wheel flanges sliding noisily on the rails.

They rolled off the turntable and out through the engine doors. Linscott was on the downtrack switches; he threw the first one as they approached it, so that the Baldwin veered onto the main Springwood spur. When they cleared the second switch, Maxon could see the rest of the townspeople strung out on the west side of the right-of-way, their bodies outlined by the hellish glow of the fire. He jerked his eyes away from the front glass, dragged his free arm across his sweating face, and swung around to the tender for another scoop of coal.

Linscott came running up alongside the cab as Staggers slammed the throttle shut and notched open the reverse lever between his knees. The old Baldwin shuddered, came to a stop for an instant with smoke feathering back from its stack, and then began to grind backward.

"Ed," Linscott shouted, "what about those two boxcars? They're blocking the tracks; you can't get around them to the coaches on the siding. Push them out of the way or couple them on and then pick up the coaches?"

"We haven't got any time to waste," Staggers yelled down to him. "We'll have to take the boxcars with us. Couple 'em on!"

TWENTY-SEVEN

From the south side of the yard, where he was clustered with the other villagers, Hannigan watched through teary eyes as the old steam locomotive reversed its course and headed uptrack to the two sealed boxcars. Smoke belched out of its stack, blended with the sooty pall that undulated across the sky. It seemed to be moving without sound, like something in a blurred silent movie, rendered mute at this distance by the roar of the blaze.

The fire was awesome now. The slopes and ridges to the west, north, and east were solid masses of flame or embers; red-tipped tongues licked at the backs of the buildings along Main Street; the grass in the village green had already been blackened and most of the oak trees had blazing crowns. Holocaust—one almost Biblical in its intensely destructive force. It made him feel as though the entire world were being systematically incinerated.

The wind and heat beat against his face. The smoke not only stung his eyes but swelled his throat and made breathing painful, as if he were trying to draw a fiery semisolid matter into his lungs; nausea surged thinly into the back of his throat. All around him men and women and children were coughing, gagging, retching.

And one of those bent double a few paces away, he realized abruptly, was Regina.

He went to her, took her shoulders gently and held her until she was able to stop dry-retching and straighten up. When she looked at him, he saw that her eyes were dulled with pain and fear, her face streaked with dried perspiration and dried tears. A tenderness welled up inside him, so acute that it became a physical ache. He had to will himself not to pull her close, hold his body against hers like a shield.

"Regina," he said.

She stepped back out of his grasp. "Please, Steve—don't."

It was almost the same thing she had said to him when he'd half-dragged her here from the roundhouse and then tried to find comforting words to say to her. And she did the same thing now that she'd done then: moved away from him and stared uptrack at the roundhouse. But he knew she wasn't watching what was happening, so much as looking for her husband. Looking for him and wondering what he was doing, what had made him follow Staggers and the others inside.

Worrying about him because she still loved him after all?

Hannigan's hands clenched. He felt impotent, frustrated, tight-drawn. He couldn't hate Maxon now—for God's sake, the man must have gone into the roundhouse because he wanted to help—and yet Maxon still stood between Regina and him. And Maxon was up there doing something, contributing, while Hannigan was waiting here passively.

I should have gone into the roundhouse, too, he thought. I should have tried to help. But what could he have done? He knew a good deal about railroading, only none of his knowledge had been gained through practical experience; Ed Staggers and the other men, including Maxon, despite his handicap, were skilled at their jobs. He would only have gotten in the way.

Hannigan looked uptrack again, past Regina's rigid form. Silhouetted against the smoky firelight, the locomotive was coupling on to the forward of the two boxcars. He could see one man working there, another man running toward the switches on the siding with the coaches, Ed Staggers leaning out of the cab. Staggers. There couldn't be a better man in charge—that was the main thing, damn it, the only important thing right now. Ed had spent his entire life on and around trains, and he had already proved that he was capable of an iron will and a clear head in a crisis like this. If anyone could get them out of here alive, Staggers was that man.

But Hannigan couldn't just keep on standing there, wanting to act, wanting to go to Regina, not being able to do either of those things. He had to move, do *something*. He turned, coughing, trying not to gag, and started down along the tracks. Some of the villagers were kneeling or sitting on the dusty ground; others were jackknifed forward at the waist, racked by fits of coughing or attacks of nausea. Melissa Logan leaned over beside her husband and vomited suddenly at his feet. One of Jack Bennett's young daughters screamed hysterically in his arms. The edge of panic, dulled by the hope that Staggers had given them, was beginning to sharpen again as the seconds ticked away and the smoke and heat intensified and the fire closed in around them.

Hannigan saw the two dark-clad strangers standing apart from everyone else, remembered that the short one, Roy, was a pyrophobe. Roy still seemed to be frozen catatonically. His gaze was riveted on the inferno along the eastern slope. His mouth hung open and a thin, glistening trail of saliva or vomit ran from one corner of it down over his chin and onto the front of his sweater. He was coughing steadily, with sounds that were like the barks of an old dog. The other stranger stood with his knuckles against his thighs, and on his face was an expression that might have been a mixture of rage and the same kind of helplessness that was inside Hannigan.

The lean one became aware that Hannigan was looking at him, met his eyes for a moment, and then deliberately shifted his body around and walked over closer to the tracks. Hannigan frowned, started after him, changed his mind when he remembered something else: he hadn't seen Henry Johnston anywhere among the villagers, hadn't seen him at all tonight.

He noticed Fred Oldaker, the night gatekeeper at the mill, down on one knee nearby. Went over to him, helped him up. "Fred," he said, "what happened to Johnston?"

Oldaker looked at him in a half-stunned way, said between coughs, "The old man? Christ, I don't know. Isn't he here?"

"No. Could the explosion have gotten him?"

"Maybe. But he was inside his house not long before it happened. Called down with instructions to open up for that truck."

"A delivery at two A.M.?"

"It's happened before."

"How many men were in the truck when it pulled up?"

"Just one."

"A short round guy?"

"Yeah."

"Did you see anybody over by the fuel tank?"

"No," Oldaker said. "Everything was quiet, then there was this funny kind of chattering noise and the tank just blew."

"Chattering noise?"

"Sounded like a rivet gun." Oldaker blinked at him. "For God's sake, Steve, why are you—"

He didn't finish what he was about to say, because a sudden shout went up from among the townspeople nearest the roundhouse. Somebody yelled hoarsely, "They're coming! They're coming!"

Hannigan swung around, and the things Oldaker

had told him were crowded into the back of his mind. Uptrack, the locomotive, its headlight glaring like a giant's eye through the roiling smoke, was on its way out of the siding with the two boxcars and the two coaches coupled on behind.

TWENTY-EIGHT

When the old Baldwin cleared the open siding switch onto the main spur, Staggers opened the throttle another notch with his left hand and then dropped the hand immediately to the knob of the air-brake lever inside its slotted disk. He put his head out the side window, looked back along the string. Linscott and Baker were hanging out on that side, one standing on the coupler knuckles between the second boxcar and the first coach, the other on the plates between the coaches. They both swung their free arms high over their heads to let him know everything was all right back there.

Staggers brought his head back inside the cab, craned his neck to look past the throttle bar at Jim Maxon. With the firebox full for the moment, Maxon was sitting on the cab seat, resting, his body bent forward tensely. His face, backlit by the glow of firelight, looked grim and strong and capable.

Staggers nodded to himself. He had had to make a snap judgment about Maxon in the roundhouse. Was a one-legged man with steam-engine experience a better risk than a two-legged man who didn't know anything about running a hog like the Baldwin? Could Maxon handle the job mentally as well as physically? The answer to the first question had been yes, because even if Maxon had trouble maintaining his balance when the Baldwin began to pitch and sway under a full head of steam, Staggers could turn the throttle over to him and tend to the firebox himself—something he wouldn't dare to do if any of the others failed to cut it as fireman. The answer to the second question had been yes, too. Jim had been half a man for the past six months, all right, not because he'd lost his leg, but because he'd let himself lose two things a lot more important: his perspective and his self-respect. The tragedy tonight seemed to have snapped him out of it, at least for the time being. What Staggers had seen when he stared into Maxon's eyes was determination, a sense of involvement and commitment, and that had been enough to sway him. Was still enough now to reaffirm his decision.

He smothered a cough, ducked his face against his shirt front, and squinted through the front glass panel. They were steaming past the roundhouse now. Ahead, the bulk of the townspeople were packed together in a long, ragged queue, moving, gesturing urgently; a few of them had splintered off and were half-staggering uptrack toward the oncoming locomotive. The fire had surged beyond them to the west, was beginning to race through the southern end of the valley. All of the buildings and all of the parked cars and pickups along Main Street and Mill Street, as well as most of the houses and property on both sides of Spruce Road, were burning. Staggers forced himself not to think about his own house, his possessions, everything he and Martha had in the world except their lives. Concentrated instead on the thought that they were just going to get out of here in time. In another few minutes the rail tracks through the pass between the southern slopes would be blocked by converging walls of flame. And inside a half hour there wouldn't be much left of Logspur except charred and flaming rubble.

But getting clear of the valley didn't end the threat to them, not by a long shot. They still had to run a twelve-mile gauntlet of dense forest land, still had to cross small wooden bridges over creek beds and washes and the old wooden trestle that spanned the Miwok River. The more momentum the fire gained, the faster it would spread. When it got hot enough it would hurl whole trees, like gigantic torches, a mile or more ahead of it, build enough speed so that even a train would be hard-pressed to outrun it. The Forestry Service would have been alerted to the blaze by now and before long there would be fire lines set up outside Springwood, air tankers aloft to bomb the fire with borate chemicals. With enough planes and fire fighters and ground equipment and a break or shift in the wind currents, they would probably be able to save Springwood—but they wouldn't be able to do much to save an old steam locomotive pulling two heavily loaded boxcars and two coaches jammed with eighty men, women and children. Not in those first eight to ten crucial miles of tinder-dry wilderness, at least.

The old Baldwin was something else to worry about. She ran along fine at low speeds, with gentle handling; but he was going to have to push her most of the way now, keep the steam up to its full working pressure of two hundred pounds as long as the water lasted. Aged and little-used rods and valves might blow, the boiler might blow, a dozen other things could strand or wreck them . . .

Staggers shook himself. No use in dwelling on what could go wrong. Thinking too much at a time like this did nothing except distract you from the job you had to do.

The Baldwin's blunt nose was coming in on the first of the running villagers. The headlamp bathed them and the clustered line of the others beyond in a smoky white glare. Staggers closed the throttle, jerked the whistle pull to signal Linscott and Baker, who were manning the hand brakes on the converted caboose, and then worked the air-brake lever. He saw the rest of the townspeople surge toward him in a body, some of them with their mouths open, making sounds that he could barely hear for the hoarse intake of the air pump, the low shriek of the brake shoes binding against wheel rims, the constant barking of the exhaust. Then the Baldwin was past them all, and he brought it to a hard, jolting stop.

He set the brakes, swung off his cab seat. "Stay put and watch the firebox," he called to Maxon, and caught the side bulkhead and levered himself out through the gangway. Dropped down to the dusty ground amid thin jets of steam.

A wave of heat and acrid smoke buffeted him; his lungs convulsed and he was racked with a fit of coughing. He dragged his handkerchief out, held it up to his mouth, and started uptrack to where the villagers were massed at the darkened cars. Stopped abruptly, relieved, when he saw that they weren't fighting each other, that they were still keeping their heads—letting the women and children in first. Steve Hannigan seemed to have taken charge, and Linscott and Baker and Bud Franklin were helping him hand people up the portable side steps on each of the two coaches. Steam and smoke swirled around them, half-obscured the tracks and the yard and the round-house.

Staggers retreated, climbed up onto the running board again and hung there looking back. All of the women and children were aboard now; the men were beginning to clamber in after them. Over on Mill Street there was a dull, booming explosion—a second, a third. Automobile gas tanks erupting. Fire and smoke gouted upward; falling sparks lashed the roundhouse roof, spotting it with flame.

When there were fewer than twenty men left outside, Staggers put his handkerchief away and pushed back up onto the cab deck. Maxon was stoking again; the butterfly doors on the firebox were open and his bent-backed frame was limned in the bright ruddy glow of the coals. Staggers slid his buttocks onto the seat, peered through the side window to the south. The fire fronts were converging rapidly on the low granite walls of the pass—too rapidly. Christ. But we've still got time, he thought. We're still going to make it.

But it was going to be close.

He laid his hand on the air-brake lever, muscles knotted and aching with tension, and took a look back at the rear. The last few of the men were just disappearing inside the coaches. A moment later he saw Hannigan lean out of the forward one, Lee Adcock out of the converted caboose. Both of them signaled with frantic waves of their arms.

Staggers pulled the whistle, released the brakes, and opened the throttle.

The Baldwin jerked, began to roll again. Couplers

banged and rods clanked and smoke barked from the stack. Watching the steam gauge, he opened her out one notch, two, three—felt her begin to hum and roar around him, creating a thunderous pulse that drowned out the thrumming of the fire. His blood began to pump faster, as it always did when he was at the throttle of a big steam hog like this one and she was beginning to run. He gritted his teeth, put his head out the window again to stare downtrack.

The end of the yards loomed ahead. Beyond, to the west, where the last of the village homes were located, the fire had churned to within seventy-five yards of the right-of-way. And on the east side, the rolling meadow land that stretched away to the pass was sheeted with flame all the way down to within twenty yards of the tracks. The pass's fractured rock walls a hundred yards ahead shone a pulsing reflected red, like superheated metal in a forge.

Staggers opened the throttle another notch and watched the flames and the glowing walls hurtle toward them.

TWENTY-NINE

Zacharias was thrown back hard against the cracked leather seat when the train jerked into motion, then thrown hard forward and to the right as the coach shuddered and swayed. His shoulder jarred into Tully, sitting next to him at the window, and Tully made a grunting noise but didn't look at him. Didn't even turn his head from the window glass and the fire raging outside.

The train picked up speed. Zacharias grabbed on to the seat in front of him, steadied himself as the coach began to vibrate. Glass panes rattled, the floorboards and walls creaked and chattered. Firelight flickered through the car, created twisting shadow patterns that gave the people around him an unreal, nightmare kind of look. Some of the kids were still wailing, some of the women sobbing, everybody else choking and gasping.

There were burns on his arms and legs, on his face, on his scalp—none of them serious, but all of them working together to make his body ache and sting. But at least the smoke and the heat weren't so bad in here. Not yet, anyway. He could almost breathe again without pain and he didn't feel as if he were going to puke at any second, the way he had outside.

He tried to pull his thoughts together, but his head just wasn't working the way it should. He'd never been afraid of much and he wasn't afraid now. Yet a thing like that fire out there, the way it moved and ran crazy wild—he couldn't seem to come to grips with it. He felt confused, powerless, as if he didn't have any control of his life any more. Out of his element, that was why, a part of things he didn't understand: a mob of country people, a rattletrap old train, a forest fire.

Then there was Tully. Tully had always been a cool head, dependable, every inch a pro. But the way he was now, Zacharias didn't know him at all. His hang-up about fire was so strong he was like a zombie. He couldn't think or talk; he didn't even know where he was. If he stayed that way until they got clear, it wouldn't make any difference; but what if he panicked the way he had at the intersection, before Zacharias could stop him—did something or said something that would blow the idea they were truckers? Zacharias had tried to talk to him while they were waiting beside the tracks, make him understand what had happened inside the mill compound, snap him out of it. But Tully'd just stood there, staring at the fire. Hadn't even moved when he started coughing or when he puked on himself—just stood there and puked on himself like a skid row rummy. If Zacharias had been able to do it he'd have put Tully's lights out for good, because it was the only sure way to protect himself; he still had the silenced Woodsman tucked down inside his pants. The only thing he could think to do instead was to wet-nurse Tully along, watch him every second and make sure none of these people got close to him. Particularly that big red-headed guy up in the front part of the car, the one who'd helped him get away from the mill. Zacharias didn't like the way that one kept looking at them, as if he were getting ideas.

The train continued to gather speed and the coach kept on rocking and swaying. Then the flickering light inside got brighter, lit up the whole car, and all at once the people on the left-hand side began crying out. Zacharias looked over that way, and there was nothing outside the windows except fire. Up close, not more than a few yards away.

He held on to the seat in front of him, and he could feel his scrotum shriveling. One of the kids screamed. Tully swiveled around beside him, leaned across in front of his body so that Zacharias was able to smell the hot puke-sour odor of his breath—

And the forward windows darkened suddenly to a

dull red glow; all the windows darkened, like a chain of lights going out one by one. The dancing shadows deepened, took over the car again. Outside the windows Zacharias saw rock, walls of jagged bare rock. He let out an explosive breath, heard the same relieved sound magnified all around him, and his body sagged backward against the seat. Dripping sweat blurred his eyes; he let go of the seat back and swiped at them with his sweater sleeve.

Jesus!

Tully was still leaning forward beside him, hands splayed out on his knees. There were no more flames for him to watch, but he looked as if he were still seeing them: the one eye nearest Zacharias bulged, glistened, seemed as big around as the bottom of a water glass. He was breathing very fast, his mouth wide open, caked with dried drool and sweat and vomit.

Viciously Zacharias shoved him away, threw him against the window. Tully blinked once, out of focus, and then turned his head and pressed his face up close to the glass. Put one hand flat against the rattling pane and made a grunting, muttering sound low in his throat. Began to stir around on the seat, like maybe he was starting to regain some of his senses.

Zacharias stared at him. If Tully panicked again, he'd have to cold-cock him. He should have done that back in the yard, for Christ's sake, while nobody was paying attention to them. He'd been thinking straight, that's just what he'd have done.

Shit, what a mess. What a lousy fucking mess. No ordnance, a quarter of a million dollars blown to hell, Johnston and Frame blown to hell, Tully a threat instead of an ally, that gut-wrenching wildfire burning all around them. Frame's fault, goddamn him. Why had he done it? Why?

Why had that stupid nigger used the Thompson gun?

THIRTY

The last Regina saw of the valley, the last she would ever see of it, was the homes burning along its southern perimeter. Somewhere in the mass of flames was her home, hers and Jim's, and as the train plunged ahead between the pass walls, she felt a terrible sense of loss. A substantial and material part of her life had ended tonight, and she could never reclaim it. But she also felt a kind of spiritual release that, oddly, carried with it little grief or pain. It was as if she had been displaced in time as well as space, hurled forward to an uncertain future which would bear little resemblance to her past. As if all her bridges had literally been burned behind her.

She turned her head from the window, looked down at her lap. Her hands moved there; she could not seem to keep them still. Her fingers felt dry, papery, when she rubbed them together, vaguely numb in the knuckles and joints. The same vague numbness seemed to have gotten into her mind too, giving her thoughts a detachment that was almost dreamlike. Maybe that was why she had that feeling of displacement. Maybe it was.

The train was going very fast now and the car pitched, rolled, made loud vibrating sounds as if it would shake itself apart. Only nothing like that would happen, she told herself. Ed Staggers knew what he was doing. And Jim knew what he was doing, too—at least right now he did, up there as fireman in the cab. Lloyd Tyrell had told her when she'd boarded the car where Jim was and what he was doing. Tyrell had sounded surprised by the fact, but Regina had not been. Her surprise had come earlier, when Jim ran suddenly to the roundhouse after the other men, because she had considered him to be so eaten away inside by his bitterness that he was incapable of positive action. As had Tyrell and probably everyone else. That was why, confused, she had reacted as she had outside the roundhouse, trying to stop him. It was only later that she had accepted the truth—only later that she felt the tentative stirrings of hope for him.

But would it last? That was the question. Would it last—and would he need and want her again if it did?

Shimmering light began to illuminate the windows, to fill the car again. Regina raised her head to look out on one side and then the other. The rock walls had slid past; they were clear of the pass now. The hillside to the east was blanketed in smoke and flame; that to the west, parallel to the train, hadn't started to burn yet, but when she edged around to look behind them, she saw fire flowing in vast surflike waves down the ridge above the pass. A tremor went through her. She turned her eyes back to her shaking hands, watching them flutter against each other. Listened to the fast rhythmic pounding of the wheels and the painful human sounds that surrounded her.

After a moment she sensed Steve Hannigan looking at her across the lurching aisle. Did not raise her head this time. She knew what would be in his face, his eyes, shining like visual echoes of the words he had spoken to her that night, and she didn't want to see it again now.

Jim. And Steve.

Which one?

I don't know, she thought. This isn't the time for decisions like that; we may all be killed.

And yet she was beginning to understand at a deeper level of perception that, no matter what, she had already made her decision. She knew exactly which of them it had to be, and it would not be long before she would finally have to admit it to herself.

THIRTY-ONE

Maxon finished shoveling the firebox full again, checked the steam—holding at one-eighty—and sank onto the fireman's seat to rest and mop sooty sweat from his face. His back was stiff from the twisting and bending; the stump of his right leg throbbed with pain. The air was clogged with cinders and smoke, and the heat from the box and from the fire-wind was intense. His skin felt blistered, his lungs as though they were being scraped with hot sandpaper.

Staggers had the throttle wide open, and the whir of the drivers, the beat of the trucks, the houndlike bark of the exhaust created a sound in Maxon's ears like that of echoing thunder. The engine and the tender and the cars behind pitched and writhed in a constant sidewise motion. He'd managed to keep his balance so far, but he had to hang on to the seat or the bulkhead each time they nosed a curve and then swung onto the tangent again.

They were winding now across the long narrow valley south of the Logspur pass, between high ridges furred with second-growth pine and Douglas fir. The headlamp made shiny ribbons of the rails ahead, illuminated brush-laden gullies and stretches of sloping grassland along the right-of-way. So far they had outdistanced the fire to the west, although he could see the bright glow flushing the sky over there. But the fire on the east was keeping pace with them, matching their speed, as if in a kind of mad race. Firebrands hurtled forward through the pall of smoke like comet's tails. Sparks and flame fountained up ahead of them on that side—the same side where the tracks would eventually hook around and climb up between a cut in the long eastern ridge.

He leaned forward, bracing himself, and called to Staggers on the high seat opposite, "Gaining on us to the east, Ed."

"Yeah," Staggers called back, "I see it."

"Try for more steam?"

"No. Safety valves are starting to pop now."

Maxon knew he was right, slammed his fist against the front paneling in frustration. He could hear the valves popping and cracking, and the old cylinders and drivers had already begun to labor. He watched Staggers shut down the steam a little to relieve some of the boiler pressure, heard the popping diminish almost instantly, and raised his head to look through the side glass again.

The forward line of the fire was gaining on them.

They were nearing the end of the valley; ahead the tracks made a long thirty-degree curve to the east, and on the far side of the bend there was a short wooden bridge spanning a dry wash. Maxon's body tensed as they started through the curve, as Staggers kicked in a few pounds of air to take out the wobble, kicked the brakes on lightly and then kicked them off again. But when they cut the segments and came onto the tangent he saw that the bridge was all right; the sparks and the firebrands hadn't gotten to it yet.

After they clattered across the bridge the fire was almost in front of them, sweeping toward the right-of-way less than a thousand yards above. The heat grew even more intense, dried his sweat the instant it came out of his pores; the hot smoke flooding his lungs made him feel light-headed, dizzy. The tracks began to climb gradually toward the ridge cut, but the cut itself and the line through it were obscured. All he could see was rolling smoke and spear-tips of flame, and above that, in the far distance, the pine-dark summits of the Trinity Alps silhouetted against the red-black sky.

A hundred yards ahead something suddenly came running out of the twisting gray mass—something alive and on fire. A deer, a six-point buck. It staggered as it came on the rails, began to run around in pain-maddened circles, and finally toppled over, dead or dying. The flames turned it black and shapeless in the moment before the locomotive lunged past it. Maxon's stomach heaved. He could smell, or thought he could smell, the sickening half-sweet odor of burning hair and cooking flesh.

Their speed decreased as the grade steepened. Staggers opened the steam again and the engine and the cars bucked, jolted, regained some of the lost momentum. Cinders from the belching stack fell beside the cab like thin black rain. Visibility ahead was less than a hundred yards and closing.

Maxon squinted at the steam gauge, pushed off the seat and staggered, choking and gasping, to the tender. Braced himself against its bulkhead and shoveled more coal. A wave of nausea hit him as he turned back to the firebox, nearly made him black out. For the first time, his artificial leg slipped on the cab deck, pitched him off balance against the seat, and he went down hard beside it on his left buttock.

Lumps of coal bounced and rattled through the cab like marbles in a shaken box. The impact with the deck had jarred him, chased away some of the nausea. He groped for the shovel, found it, drove the handle hard against his stump; the pain cleared the rest of the dizziness from his mind. He managed to grab the seat and haul himself erect.

Staggers was looking across at him. Between hacking coughs that bent him forward he called, "You all right, Jim?"

Maxon gestured that he was, pawed at his stinging eyes, and twisted around again to the tender. Got another shovelful of coal and this time made it to the firebox without stumbling. He opened the butterfly doors and fed the blaze inside.

Outside the cab, the smoke flowed around them, seemed to envelop the train. It was as if they were struggling blindly upward through a kind of poisonous gray gelatin. Panic clawed at Maxon. They couldn't keep breathing much longer in thick smoke like this; they'd both pass out. Runaway train then, derailment on one of the downslope curves, the wreck and the fire would get them all . . .

Seconds that seemed like minutes crawled away.

Then, abruptly, the laboring upward pull of the engine ceased; the Baldwin rocked and the front box-car banged against the tender as she leveled out, surged ahead. The smoke on Maxon's side of the cab began to shred. He blinked, scraped at his eyes, blinked again—and had an impression of jagged slabs and ribs of granite rock in the smoke rifts.

The cut; they were into the ridge cut.

God, he thought, and dragged his head around to peer blearily at Staggers. The old man was bent double on the high seat, still coughing in spasms, and his face was a glowing sooty bronze in the light from the cab lamp. But he was all right: his teeth were bared and his left hand was wrapped around the throttle, shutting it down a notch to even out their speed when they started on the downslope run.

Maxon clung to the bulkhead. The smoke in front of them was breaking up, too, and the brightening glare of the headlight showed him part of the tracks ahead, the wooded slopes to the west and the high rock shoulder to the east. The terrible blasts of heat had lessened. There was oxygen in the air again; the sweetness of it in his heaving lungs made his knee feel weak.

They pounded through the cut and headed into the descent on the far grade. Maxon pushed along the bulkhead to the gangway, leaned out to look behind them. There was no sign of flames on any of the cars in the string—none of the flying sparks and burning cinders had settled on them. Wildfire swept all along the northeast rim and on the ridges and hollows well beyond. But to the southeast, paralleling the right-of-way, ragged granite formations and volcanic earthflows stretched out and down for at least a third of a mile. Madrone and salmonberry shrubs and a few pines grew there—too sparsely for the fire to take much hold. That section of terrain wouldn't check the onrushing flames for long, but maybe long enough for the train to clear the trestle across the Miwok River, three miles down the line.

When they nosed into the first of the downslope curves, he hobbled back to the firebox and looked at the steam. Holding. The grade wasn't steep enough here for Staggers to have to use the brakes, but he had his hand on the lever anyway. He had opened the side window again, and hot streaming air, half-smoky and half-fresh, swirled through the cab.

Staggers hawked deep in his throat and spat phlegm through the window. Then he called hoarsely, "Cars okay on your side?"

"Look to be."

"Thank God. It was close back there."

"Yeah. But we're going to make it now."

Staggers grimaced. "We've got a long way to go yet."

"The river'll slow the fire up on the west," Maxon said. "We can outrun it pretty easy from there; it's less than seven miles to Springwood."

The old man didn't respond. He sat very still for a moment, staring at nothing, as if he were thinking ahead, worrying. Or praying.

They came through the first curve, wound into the second. The grade began to level off. Maxon looked at the steam again, saw that it was dropping a little, and caught up the shovel and swiveled to the tender. The heat from the ballast lashed at him when he pedaled open the firebox doors, and a hot coal fragment popped out and stung his right cheek, dropped to the front of his shirt. He didn't take the time to slap at the smoldering cloth until he'd fed in the shovelful of coal and was turning back to the tender for another.

At the bottom of the grade the tracks hooked south-east around the long section of rock, then looped back to the southwest across a series of hillocks and short, shallow vales. By the time they were halfway across, less than two miles from the river, the fire to the east had dropped well back—but the west fire was coming on fast, closing in on them. Maxon could see billows of smoke and leaping vanguards of flame beyond the right-hand gangway, as near to the tracks as five hundred yards in spots.

He thought about the trestle, as Staggers must have been doing all along, and an icy desperation came into him. The trestle was built almost entirely of old wooden beams, and it would take only one small fire-brand to torch it off, within minutes to burn it like kindling and turn it into a collapsing black skeleton. The drought had reduced the river to a sluggish trickle; it flowed a hundred feet below ground level, between sheer rock walls that were impossible to scale. If the trestle was burning when they got to it, they would have nowhere to go.

He remembered the burning deer that had come running out to the right-of-way earlier, the way it had died, the stench of its cooking flesh. And shuddered. And took the shovel back to the tender even though the steam was up again and the firebox was nearly full.

The Baldwin thundered ahead, shuddering from side to side as if it were trying to break loose from the rails. The safety valves were making intermittent popping noises again, but Staggers didn't shut down the steam this time, not yet. And Maxon didn't quit shoveling; he kept the box full and the ballast at white heat.

One mile to the river now.

One mile to the old wooden trestle.

THIRTY-TWO

Tully couldn't see the flames any more—and inside his head his father stopped screaming.

His father was dead and they'd put him out; the fire was out.

The images of that night long ago faded; he felt a sudden mental jarring. Thoughts began to tumble together; his senses began to work again all at once. Pain in his chest, the sour taste of vomit in his mouth, the sounds of coughing and crying and metal grinding on metal like a throbbing rhythm in his ears. He blinked several times, realized with dull amazement that he was sitting in a shadowed, swaying, speeding railroad car with dozens of other people, with somebody beside him that he recognized abruptly as Zacharias. He couldn't remember coming in here, couldn't remember anything about a train. All he remembered, and that only in a vague way, was somebody grabbing him away from the car at the village intersection, and then Zacharias slapping him. There was nothing else in his memory but the fire, fire everywhere, and his father screaming and dying while he and his mother looked on.

133

He tried to make words, to say something to Zacharias, but his jaw only flapped mutely. When Zacharias saw him doing that, his eyes narrowed and his face—burned face, hair singed off, Jesus—got tight. He caught Tully's arm, held it in a hard grip.

"You coming out of it?" Zacharias said under his breath. "You know who I am?"

Tully managed a convulsive nod.

"All right then, listen to me. We're on a train, the people in the village put a train together, and we got out of there. We're clear of the village; we're heading for Springwood. You understand?"

Tully understood. But there was dim flickering light in the car, firelight in the car, and a haze of smoke. He swiveled his head to the window, stared out. Smoke all over the sky. And flames, he could see the flames again—

Zacharias' hand caught his sweater, jerked him around roughly. "Don't look out there. Just stay cool; we're going to be okay."

He tried again to talk, finally got words out in a voice that cracked and didn't sound like his own. "Mel . . . Christ, Mel, it's still there, it's coming. . . ."

"It won't get us, goddamn it. It hasn't got us yet and it's not going to."

Tully started to tremble. He wanted to look out at the fire, didn't want to look at it, had to look at it, wouldn't look at it. The panic stirred in him, but it stayed down below the surface of his mind like an undertow.

"Bend forward and put your head down on your knees," Zacharias said. "I don't want you looking out the window any more."

"Mel . . ."

"Do it!"

Tully did it. He closed his eyes, but as soon as he did that the rocking motion of the car, the smell of smoke, made him dizzy and sick to his stomach. He popped them open again, gagged but didn't vomit.

Zacharias leaned down close beside him. "Now stay that way. Don't raise up until I tell you to and don't say anything—not now and not when we get to Springwood. I'll do the talking for both of us. Understand?"

"I understand," Tully said.

"All right."

He sat there with his cheek resting on one knee, hands clasped on the back of his head. The noise and the motion blended together to dull and jumble his thoughts again. Clear of the village, heading for Springwood. Fire coming outside, but it hadn't gotten them yet, and it wasn't going to. Wasn't going to get him the way it had his father. Wouldn't let it, wouldn't die like that.

In the back of his mind his father shrieked again, just once, and he saw the hungry flames.

The panic rippled, tugged harder.

THIRTY-THREE

Sitting on the aisle across from Regina, Hannigan kept watching her and, beyond her, through the windows, the advancing fire and smoke. Her head was bowed and she was motionless except for her hands: they twitched continually against each other in a chain of paroxysms. She had been sitting like that for twenty minutes; she'd even sat like that all the way through the climb to the ridge cut a little while ago, when the smoke outside had surrounded the car and come streaming into it like gas into an oven and half-suffocated them for long agonizing seconds. She seemed dazed, not quite functioning mentally.

God, how he wanted to go to her.

He'd almost done it when the smoke enveloped them. It had seemed for an instant that they wouldn't get through it, and if they were about to die he wanted Regina in his arms when it happened; he'd lurched, choking, to his feet and started over. Only then they had reached the top of the grade, and the smoke had started to break up outside, and it became more important as they plunged downslope to keep the others calm and conscious, to go back through the car shouting at them to open windows a little so that crosscurrents of wind could air it out.

Now he was just sitting again, watching Regina and the fire, waiting—and the feeling of impotency lay like a heavy solid mass in the pit of his stomach.

But the brief sense of fatalism was gone: it looked as though they had a better-than-even chance of making it now. The fire to the east was behind them and they were staying out in front of the blaze on the west. It couldn't be much longer before they reached the Miwok River trestle, and once they were over it the worst part of the trip figured to be over.

Still, he knew any number of things could keep them from reaching Springwood. The fire could surge ahead of them if the wind picked up, cut them off. Staggers was pushing that old locomotive at top speed, and the old man had told him more than once that she was about ready for retirement from active duty. Despite the care he'd given her, the Baldwin's operating parts were aged and worn; she might not be able to hold up under this kind of strain. And the same might be true of the villagers. The inpouring smoke on the grade had half-panicked them. Two of the women and three of the children had blacked out briefly, and several others were on the verge of hysteria. If they had another close call, there was no telling what might happen inside the coach.

Hannigan thought about the pyrophobic stranger, Roy. The man had still been catatonic when Hannigan had gone through the car earlier, but he could come out of it at any time—the blind panic could take hold of him again. He edged around on his seat to look back toward Roy's seat. Couldn't see Roy at first, just the other one sitting on the aisle. Then, as the car swayed and jounced, he had an impression of a hunched back, hands clasped over the back of a head: Roy leaning forward, maybe being sick.

He studied the lean man for a few seconds. That one was staring straight ahead, with no expression on his face, but still looking tense and hard-edged in the shadowy glow of the fire. Tough type, Hannigan thought. A little dangerous, somehow, the kind of man you wouldn't want to pick a fight with because he'd be capable of hurting you badly, maybe even killing you.

Hannigan had known truckers like that in the past—but *was* the lean one a trucker? Two o'clock in the morning was a damned funny hour for truckers to be delivering goods of any kind. He thought again of what Fred Oldaker had told him: Roy had been the only man in the double-trailer rig when it pulled up to the mill gate. Neither Roy nor the truck had gone inside the compound before the explosion, but the lean man *had* been inside, had come running out from the direction of the burning fuel tank. How had he gotten in? What had he been doing in there?

And that chattering noise Oldaker had heard—had the stranger somehow been responsible for the explosion? He'd been close enough to it to get his hair singed off and his face and clothing burned.

And what had happened to Henry Johnston?

Hannigan didn't like the implications of all that. But he couldn't put it together so it made any kind of sense. The two strangers could conceivably be thieves, yet he couldn't imagine anything at the mill big enough and valuable enough to require a double-trailer truck to steal it. There was also the fact that Johnston had called down to Oldaker to tell him the truck was coming, which seemed to indicate he'd known the two men, or at least who they were.

Something else jogged out of his memory: when he'd helped the lean one run clear of the mill, their bodies had touched a couple of times and Hannigan had felt a hard object along the man's side, tucked into or hanging from his belt. He hadn't thought much about it then, but now he wondered a little uneasily what the object was. A wrench or some other kind of tool, maybe. Or maybe it was something not nearly so harmless. Maybe it was a—

The locomotive's whistle began a sudden urgent wail. One long blast, three short ones.

The signal for *This train is about to stop.*

In the same instant Hannigan felt a change in the train's speed that told him the throttle had been shut down and the air brakes applied; the train seemed to hurtle onward as if it were suspended in unchecked motion, like a downhill runaway. A chill brushed his neck and he grabbed on to the seat back in front of him, turned his head to shout to the other people to brace themselves. But the shout was lost in the savage whining screech of brake shoes locking against wheel flanges as the air hose swelled full.

The coach bucked, shuddered, plowed hard against the boxcar in front of it. A few of the other people were pitched to the floorboards; there were shouts, terrified cries, the thin moaning shriek of a child. The train began a violent deceleration, so violent that Hannigan, clinging to the seat back, was afraid a coupler would snap or a wheel would be kicked loose from a rail.

And he understood then that something drastic had happened up ahead of them, because it was the emergency air that had been applied: Staggers was trying to bring the train to a full emergency stop.

THIRTY-FOUR

When the burning tree came rolling down the long rock-ribbed slope to the west, Staggers was looking straight ahead through the front glass panel—looking at the trestle. They had just come through a short curve, into a straight that was flanked on the one side by the slope and on the other by a boulder-strewn meadow, and the trestle had appeared a third of a mile downtrack. It was stained a smoky reddish color by the firelight, but there were no flames on it anywhere; it hadn't started to burn yet. A grim relief had begun to rise inside him.

Then he saw the tree.

The rock shoulder at the top of the slope was shrouded in smoke—a firebrand had landed up there minutes ago, torched off the front line of pines along the crown—and the burning tree burst down out of the smoke, scattering dying tails of fire as it bounced and rolled toward the right-of-way, three hundred yards ahead of the Baldwin. It was a big thick-trunked pine, its boughs cinder-black and wreathed in flame, part of its decaying root system still attached: a dead tree already uprooted, dislodged by the force of the blaze or by something falling against it.

Maxon saw it at the same time, yelled words that Staggers heard but didn't listen to. Instinctively he threw the throttle shut, reached for the emergency air. The tree bounced, hit a hooked limestone ledge that acted on it as a ski-run acts on a skier, sailing it up and then down hard twenty yards from the tracks and parallel to them, amid a boiling shower of dust, loose rock, and smoky fire. But momentum kept it rolling, and for a second Staggers thought it would roll clear of the rails well before they got to that point.

Instead it jarred *between* the steel ribbons, rocked, and settled straight down along the ties as cleanly as if it had been guided and slotted there by design.

Christ Almighty! Staggers thought. He threw the emergency air wide open, bellowed "Brace yourself!" to Maxon, and yanked frantically on the whistle pull.

The turbine howled, the exhaust roared, the air pumps hammered; then the brake shoes screamed against wheel rims and sprayed thin fans of sparks.

Draft rigging buckled as the brakes held traction. Staggers had his body anchored on the seat, his feet planted on the footboard, but the shuddering slide of the locomotive, the slap of the tender and the other cars behind, rocked him anyway and banged his head against the side window frame hard enough to give him a second or two of double vision. Across the cab, Maxon was down on his good knee, clinging to the bulkhead, trying to haul himself upright.

The burning tree seemed to be rushing toward them at tremendous speed, looming massively in the white wash of light from the headlamp. Through the open window Staggers saw the yellowish flames leaping up, the bluish flames that rimmed the top of the boiler stack. There was a brassy taste in his mouth. His heart acted as though it were trying to burst through the walls of his chest.

Stop, he thought. Stop, damn you, *stop!*

The skidding part of the deceleration began to let up; the wild scream of metal on metal lessened. The old Baldwin shimmied, seemed to want to stand on its nose. In front of them the burning pine was fifty yards away, forty, thirty; Staggers couldn't see the splintered root system or the lower half of the flaming bole—

And the locomotive's nose pilot bumped against the tree with enough force to rock the cab to and fro like a toy.

And they ground to a quivering halt.

Pain erupted in Staggers' neck, gave him a fleeting fear of whiplash before it dulled and he was able to move. Steam hissed, valves popped like gunshots. There was the stench of hot metal, of wood smoke and coal smoke. He pushed off the seat, saw Maxon leaning against the bulkhead with his face pinched and bloodless beneath its coating of soot and dried sweat, but he didn't waste any time with words. He stumbled straight to the gangway, swung out and down, and ran to where he could see the front of the Baldwin.

The fire-streaked pine was still jammed squarely between the rails, fifteen feet forward of the pilot.

Bastard!

He looked at the trestle, and it was still clear of fire. Swung his gaze to the rocky incline. There weren't any flames on the slope itself, nothing there to have caught fire in the path of the burning pine—but flames licked upward through the thick smoke haze across the crown, several hundred yards back, and in spots on the barren, humped-up ground that stretched down to the rim of the river gorge. He pivoted, looked to the east. The blaze hadn't gotten to the boulder-strewn meadow on that side, but it was sweeping fast over the hills behind it.

Staggers dragged smoky air into his lungs, ran back to where Maxon was hanging out of the gangway. Linscott and Baker, he saw, were pounding toward the Baldwin from the rear of the train; a few of the other townspeople had their heads poked out of the coach windows. He could hear the faint, high-pitched babble of their voices above the hissing steam and the complaining engine and the distant humming crackle of the fire.

Maxon yelled down to him, "Ed—can we kick it clear?"

"No. It's still sitting smack between the rails."

Linscott shouted, "What's happened, for God's sake?" as he and Baker came running up, but Staggers didn't answer him. His mind sorted furiously through possible options. They couldn't push the tree all the way across the trestle, even if they put out the fire on it. Take too long: that was a damn big pine, the Baldwin was already close to overheating, and the trestle was liable to go before they could get across. Only one thing to do, then. Take some time to do that, too, but not as much.

He shouted to the others, "We'll have to move it by hand—get the top section canted crosstrack enough so I can nose it clear."

"By hand?" Linscott said. He was staring downtrack at the burning pine. "Ed, that's a big mother—"

"I don't care how big it is, there're forty men with strong backs on this train." But as he said that, something else occurred to him. "The boxcars," he shouted. "There's some kind of machine parts in there, might be something we can use for pry bars. Joe, you and Bake break one of the seals, see what you can find."

He pushed past them and began to run uptrack to the coaches.

THIRTY-FIVE

Zacharias stood in the car aisle, people swarming around him, and tried to shake the confusion out of his head. He didn't know what the hell had happened, none of them knew what had happened—just that they'd all of a sudden gone into a long hard-braking skid and finally come to a jolting stop that had thrown half of the others off their seats.

Outside the right-hand windows somebody started yelling, "All the men out! All the men out! Women and children stay where you are!"

Everybody kept swarming around, as confused as he was. Then, up front, the big red-haired guy shouted, "You heard him. All the men out; all the women and children stay here."

They got it together then. The women and the wailing kids sat down in their seats and the men began to push out through the entranceway. Zacharias hesitated, looked at Tully and saw that he was still sitting in the same place, holding his head where he'd cracked it on something and a bloody gash had opened up. He seemed to be out of it again—or out of it enough so he wouldn't panic and do something crazy. All right, Zacharias thought, and turned to the front and followed the rest of the men outside.

They were all running up toward the engine, and when he got there himself he saw that there was a goddamn burning tree sitting in the center of the tracks, right in front of the engine. Christ, no wonder they'd had to brake so fast and hard. If they'd hit that fucker with any speed, they'd all be dead now in the wreckage.

Smoke streamed and curled overhead, coming from the top of a long rocky slope on that side of the train; it started him coughing again. He could see fire up there sweeping toward what looked like a narrow canyon up ahead. There was a trestle across the canyon, an old *wooden* trestle, and that told him all he needed to know about the way things stood. A little shiver ran through him. Fear. He kicked it down, got a grip on himself, and paid attention to the old man, the engineer, who was standing off to one side and hollering instructions.

144

What he was saying was that they were going to move the top section of the tree so he could shove it clear with the engine. He told them to use their clothing to beat out the fire first. One of the men shouted that they couldn't move a tree that size by hand, not as hot as it was, and the old guy shouted back that somebody was opening up a boxcar to look for something they could use for pry bars.

Zacharias glanced automatically at the forward boxcar; two guys were working there, just starting to slide open the doors. Inside he could see stacks of crates and long wooden boxes stenciled with the words *Acme Foundry—Machine Parts*. And something clicked in his mind, kept him standing where he was while the others rushed ahead to the burning tree, stripping off shirts as they went.

One of the men at the boxcar climbed up inside, fumbled around a couple of the crates, and then yelled down to the other one to get him tools from the cab. The second guy ran ahead to the engine, past a young gimp with black grime all over him who was looking at Zacharias; he disappeared inside the cab. Zacharias started toward the boxcar, and the gimp limped toward him and shouted, "You! Get downtrack and help the others!"

Zacharias stopped, but he kept on looking at those crates and boxes inside the car.

The second guy came back out of the cab with a couple of claw hammers in his hand, took them to the boxcar and handed them up to the one inside. Climbed up beside him. Then each of them started popping open a crate.

"What's the matter with you?" the gimp shouted at Zacharias. "I told you to help the others!"

He didn't move.

The two men in the car got their crates open at the same time—and both of them jerked as if there were strings attached to their necks and somebody'd pulled them. One of them reached inside his crate, came up with something in his hand.

"Jesus Christ—guns! There's guns in here!"

Zacharias knew for sure then that this was what that crazy son of a bitch Johnston had done with the ordnance. The fear cut at him again. And a savage empty rage. They'd been dragging the stuff through fire and smoky heat all the way from the village, and now they were sitting here with it and the fire was closing in around them, and all it would take would be for the heat to reach a certain temperature inside one of those cars—

Riding and sitting here in the middle of a fucking time bomb . . .

THIRTY-SIX

Maxon pulled up short, forgot all about the lean stranger, and snapped around to stare disbelievingly at Linscott and Baker inside the boxcar.

"Guns!" Linscott shouted again. "That's all there is in here; the car's full of them."

God!

Behind him Staggers' voice said, "What's going on here?" and Maxon turned as the old man hurried up. "What's the matter, Jim?"

Maxon told him.

"What?"

"It's true, Ed," Linscott yelled down. "Look!"

Staggers ran over to the car, Maxon hobbling at his side. Linscott leaned down, and in his hand was a .45 caliber Army-issue automatic, brand new and shiny, glinting reddish pinpoints of firelight. "It doesn't make any sense," Linscott said. "What would old man Johnston be doing with stuff like this?"

"The hell with that," Staggers said urgently, "that's not important. What about ammunition? There live ammo in there, too?"

"Yeah," Baker said. "This crate here's jammed with .45 clips. If the heat or the fire gets to it . . ."

He didn't have to finish the sentence; they all knew what would happen if the heat or the fire got to that live ammunition. And knew, too, they were lucky it hadn't happened already—lucky they were all still alive. Maxon remembered the heat and smoke on the grade up to the ridge cut three miles back, the nearness of the fire there, and a cold, hollow sensation came into his stomach.

"What're we going to do?" Linscott asked. His voice was shaky now, and sweat glistened on his face. "We can't unload the cars; there's not enough time. And we can't uncouple them either, not without stranding the coaches."

Staggers said grimly, "Only choice we've got is to keep on going—get the hell out of the fire zone."

"What about the other men?" Maxon asked. "Do we tell them?"

"We've got to. They're having trouble moving the tree; they need something to use for leverage."

"Might be rifles in these long boxes," Baker said.

"That's what I'm thinking. Get 'em open and make

sure the weapons are unloaded. I'll handle the others."

Baker said, "Right," and he and Linscott turned immediately to lift down one of the long wooden crates.

Staggers swung around, took a step, checked himself when he saw the stranger still standing nearby. "Come on, mister," he snapped at the man, "what're you standing around for? Get down there and help with that tree."

The stranger hesitated. Then he seemed to shake himself, said, "Yeah, okay," and began to run downtrack with Staggers.

Maxon stepped back, looked uptrack behind the train. Clouds of smoke eddied around the curve several hundred yards distant: the fires on both sides of the right-of-way had joined somewhere back there. There was no immediate threat from the east yet, but to the west the flames were starting to draw dangerously close. The ridge above the rocky slope was covered with running fire.

And though he wasn't sure, he thought the wind might be picking up.

He could feel his nerves tightening; his head ached malignantly. We haven't got much time, he thought. Fifteen or twenty minutes at the outside. And the trestle could start to burn any second. . . .

He stared down at what was happening around the lodged tree. The other men had beaten the fire out— the pine was smoldering now, a charred black hulk—and they were struggling, without much success so far, to move the upper end of it. Some were kicking or tugging with shirt-wrapped hands at the blackened boughs, trying to strip them off to lighten the tree's weight. Staggers had moved in among them, and as Maxon watched, most of the men stopped working at the news of what was in the boxcars. He could hear their voices raised in alarm. But Staggers kept the situation under tight control, got all but four of them back to work within seconds. Those four he brought on the run to the open boxcar.

Maxon moved ahead to join them, saw in their faces the same emotions that must be reflected in his own. None of them said anything; there was nothing to say. Up in the car, Linscott and Baker had the lids off four of the boxes. Two were metal-lined and contained what looked to be partially assembled machine guns and forty-millimeter grenade launchers, and they'd pushed those aside because the weapons were stripped down and the components were coated with slick cosmoline. The other two crates were jammed with fully assembled Government-issue M-1 carbines packed in excelsior.

Maxon looked at the weapons with awe. God, there seemed to be enough firepower here to start a small war. Johnston was a strange, secretive man and nobody liked him much, but none of the mill people had ever imagined anything like this.

And where *was* Johnston anyway? Maxon couldn't remember seeing him in the village tonight, didn't think he was on the train. Explosion or the fire at the mill must have gotten him—and maybe it was what he deserved, doing Christ knew what with weapons like these.

Linscott and Baker were handing down the carbines now, and Maxon and Staggers passed them to the other four in turn. Each man carried an armload of half a dozen down the rails to the others. As the last one in line, Jack Bennett, stepped forward, a sudden buzzing noise started up in the sky to the south.

They all looked in that direction. The noise grew rapidly, became a throbbing roar. Planes, at least two of them. The Forestry Service had finally gotten air tankers up.

Maxon felt a surge of hope. If the pilots were flying low enough and close enough to the rail line to see the stalled train, they would bomb the fire around them. And maybe that would hold it back long enough for them to dislodge the tree and steam across the river trestle.

Bennett took his armload of rifles downtrack, and Linscott and Baker jumped down from the car to handle the last dozen themselves. The air tankers sounded close now, but Maxon couldn't see anything of them through the twisting layers of smoke. And when they finally passed over, frustration chased away the hope inside him: they were some distance off to the east.

"Damn it!" he shouted as the pounding roar decreased. "They didn't see us!"

"Too much smoke," Staggers shouted back. "Even if they had seen us, they'd have had to lay borate right on top of us to do us much good. Get these doors closed, Jim. Then go up in the cab and load the box. I'm going to oil up again."

Maxon nodded, and while Staggers ran down to the Baldwin he hurriedly pulled the boxcar doors shut. Then he stepped back, glanced uptrack at the coaches. The other stranger, the short fat one, was just stumbling out of the first car, but Maxon didn't pay much attention to him. The smoke was thickening along the rails behind the train, thickening everywhere—the women and kids had closed all the car windows—and it churned in his lungs, started him coughing in spasms again. The fire-wind blew hot against his cheeks, made them feel feverish.

He ran to the locomotive. The stump of his right leg was beginning to pain him again—sharp, biting little pulses. Ahead the rest of the men were lined up along the tree, working frantically with the carbines, digging muzzles and stocks down into the gravel between the ties. They'd managed to lever part of it up onto one of the rails. In the glare of the headlight their naked backs gleamed brassily with sweat as they strained against the dead weight. Another five minutes, maybe, and it looked as though they would have enough of it moved for the Baldwin to kick it clear.

Five minutes. And another five for everybody to get back into the cars and the train to start moving again . . .

Staggers was nowhere in sight, must have gone around to oil up on the other side of the locomotive. Maxon climbed into the cab, caught up the shovel, scooped coal from the tender. He could hear the men grunting around the pine outside, one of them shouting, "Heave! Heave!" Grunting and starting to cough and choke just as he was in the thickening smoke.

He pedaled open the firebox doors and flung the scoopful of coal inside. The ballast was mostly ash now, but it still glowed bright red and gave off searing heat against his face. Inside the box, all around them—like glimpses of hell. He shoveled again, kept on shoveling.

And tried not to think about the heat building around the munitions inside those boxcars.

THIRTY-SEVEN

Tully stood against the second boxcar like a man crucified—back flattened to the wood siding, arms straight out from his body, fingers hooked inward—and watched the fire coming for him. His father was screaming again, dying again, and he wanted to scream himself, but he had no voice. The panic surged and ebbed, surged and ebbed. Kept him standing there now as it had brought him lunging out of the coach a minute ago. He'd come to awareness again with his head hurting and blood all over his face and hands, and Zacharias was gone, all the men were gone, and the train had stopped moving. They had stopped *moving*. He'd looked out the window, and the flames were still close, still reaching for him, and he'd managed to get off his seat and out through the entranceway. Then the heat and the smoke and the nearness of the fire had driven him back against the boxcar.

Why weren't they moving? He had to make them move, had to get away before it was too late.

The panic surged again, didn't ebb this time. His legs moved, carried him sideways along the car to where it was hooked onto the first coach. He backed in against the coupler between the cars, crawled up over it on his buttocks, swung his legs down, and clawed his way around to the opposite side of the boxcar. But the fire was over there, too; it was everywhere; it was trying to surround him. He looked ahead desperately to the front of the train, saw that somebody was down on one knee beside the engine, that men farther on were doing something with a tree, or what looked like a tree.

He ran down there, looking back at the fire, shoes slipping on the gravelly, pine-needled dirt. The kneeling man heard him coming, glanced back at him, and then stood up as he neared and called something to him. But Tully couldn't hear it because the fire and the panic and his father were all screaming too loud. He stumbled past the man a couple of steps, stopped and stared at the others working around the tree. Moving it off the tracks, it was blocking the tracks; that was why the train had stopped. He blinked, realized dimly what it was they were using to move the tree. Carbines, M-1 carbines. But that didn't seem right; where would all of them have gotten weapons like that—

A hand caught his shoulder, half-spun him, and he was looking at the man who'd been kneeling beside the engine. An old man with a soot-blackened face, a face that looked charred like his father's that night in the street—dead face shining in the awful smoky light of the fire.

Help me help me help me!

Tully shook his head until the screaming faded and he could hear again, and the old man was saying, ". . . the hell have you been, mister? Why aren't you down there helping?" But Tully didn't listen to that; he had his mouth open and he was trying to make words of his own come out. Made them come out finally:

"Tell them to hurry up! The fire's coming, it's coming!"

The old man scowled. "Pull yourself together, man."

Tully said, "Goddamn you, make them hurry up!" and clutched at the old man's shirt. But the old man was strong and shoved him away angrily, with enough force to stagger him. Tully caught himself and started for him. Stopped again when the old man raised the big oilcan·he was holding in one hand, waved it like a club.

"Get back to the coach," he snapped at Tully. "Get back there and stay there, you damned coward; you're not doing anybody any good out here."

Tully had a savage urge to take the oilcan away from him, beat him down with it, make those other men hurry up himself. But a glimmer of reason kept him from doing that. The old man might be the train's engineer; and he couldn't take all of them on with an oilcan and his bare hands.

He backed away a couple of steps, in closer to the thing that held coal behind the engine. The old man glared at him for a second, then pivoted sharply and climbed up inside. Tully wanted to run, wanted the train to run—and just stood there looking at the flames. Heat blasted against his face; curling smoke made him cough and then gag. And the fire moved closer, closer, reaching out for him and making his father scream louder.

One of the men came running away from the tree, stopped outside the cab entrance. "We can't move it much farther," he shouted up. "And the heat's getting bad; those boxcars could blow any time!"

"All right," the old man's voice yelled down from inside. "Brace it so it's firm on the rail, and signal when you're ready."

"Right."

The panic clawed at Tully, started him moving

again. He backed away until he reached the end of the first boxcar.

M-1 carbines, all of them using M-1 carbines.

Those boxcars could blow any time.

Blow them up, burn them up.

Government-issue M-1 carbines.

Boxcars.

Johnston, the mill, Zacharias saying to him somewhere that the ordnance hadn't been inside the compound, supposed to be M-1s among the ordnance—

No!

No, no, no!

He spun and lunged over the coupler and ran feverishly to the doors on the first boxcar.

THIRTY-EIGHT

In the cab Staggers stood with his left hand opening and closing nervously around the throttle, listening to the air pump chug as the pressure built up again. The fire-wind and the pulsing heat of the box made it a furnace in there, and the air was foul with swirling smoke. He'd tied his handkerchief over his nose and mouth, but that didn't help much; he was beginning to feel sick and weak-kneed. He knew without thinking about it that his sixty-five-year-old body couldn't take much more of this kind of abuse.

Beside him, Maxon leaned tensely against the fireman's seat and kept an eye on the steam gauge. He'd shoveled the box full and the steam was up and they were ready to go as soon as Hannigan signaled that the men outside had firmed the position of the tree.

Staggers glanced again at the water glass. They were low on water now—the Baldwin was a thirsty old hog—and he'd have to watch their speed and the boiler-pressure gauge; the last thing he could afford to risk was a boiler explosion. He put his head out through the side window. He could see the upper half of the pine, and not much more than a third of it had been angled crossrail. So he wouldn't be able to ease up to it, lock the pilot against it and just push it off. It was liable to slide right back between the tracks. What he'd have to do would be to ram it, pray the impact widened the angle of tilt, and then ram it again immediately and hope to spin it loose. Momentum would have to do the rest.

Farther downtrack, drifting smoke obscured the trestle—but there didn't seem to be any flames on the wooden framework yet. Still, the fire was licking along the rim of the river gorge to the west, racing along the boulder-strewn meadow on the opposite side. The wind seemed to be picking up slightly, too. The trestle wasn't going to last much more than five minutes.

They were almost ready. He strained his eyes for Hannigan's signal—

Maxon shouted, "Ed!" with sudden alarm in his voice, jerked away from the fireman's seat. Staggers threw a look at him, saw him staring toward the right-side gangway, and whirled around.

The short fat stranger was coming up through the gangway with a gun in his hand.

Staggers froze and gaped at him incredulously. The man set his feet wide apart in front of the tender, pointing the automatic—a brand-new Army .45—at Staggers' stomach. *He got it from one of the boxcars, found an ammunition clip for it; he knows about the munitions.* He'd been in a bad way when Staggers had confronted him alongside the cab minutes ago, but now his face was wild, half-mad with terror. His eyes looked as though they were on fire.

He shouted, "Tell somebody to unhook those boxcars!"

Maxon said, "Jesus *Christ,* are you crazy?"

"Not going to blow me up—not me!"

Staggers could feel veins swelling in his face and neck. The incredulity in him had given way to fury, to savage urgency. And fear, too, but not of the gun or the short man's lunatic terror; fear for the safety of the others, all the women and children who were his responsibility.

"We can't uncouple, you goddamn fool!" he bellowed. "The *coaches* are back there!"

"Get those cars unhooked, get me away from here!"

"We're not leaving everybody here to save—"

"Do it, do it!"

"Go to hell!" Staggers roared and lunged forward recklessly, to slap at the gun.

The sound of the shot was deafening.

The bullet hit Staggers high on the left side of the chest, and the shock stopped him cold, straightened him up for an instant as if he'd run headlong into a wall. Then both hands came up in reflex to clap against his chest and he reeled, bounced off the firebox shield, sat down hard on the deck. He couldn't see, there was a darkness, like shutters, drawn across his eyes. But he heard the fading reverberations of the shot, shouts, scrambling movement. Felt numbness all through his upper body, pain in the center of it, pain spreading out, wetness spreading out under his clutching fingers.

Shot me, he thought. I'm shot.

Then his mind flickered, dimmed—and went black.

THIRTY-NINE

Hannigan stepped back from his position at the charred tree, threw the blackened carbine away behind him. They had the pine as firmed up on the rail as they were going to get it. Coughing, he dragged a forearm across his bleary eyes and then pulled the scorched and torn remnants of his shirt from around his hands. The hands were burned anyway from the hot wood; his shoulder was burned where he'd laid it against the trunk before the discovery of what was in the boxcars. But he barely felt the pain; his mind had blocked it out.

He turned toward the locomotive, to signal Staggers that they were ready—and saw the short stranger, Roy, just starting to swing up inside the cab.

There was something in Roy's hand—Hannigan couldn't tell what because of the roiling smoke—and warning bells clanged in his mind. He hadn't had time to think about the munitions, but he knew intuitively they had something to do with the presence of the two strangers at the mill tonight, maybe with what had happened there and with Johnston's disappearance. That made the two of them dangerous, all right, and Roy even more so because of his terror of fire. And now he had gone into the cab carrying something— something that could be a gun if he'd found out about the contents of the boxcar—

Hannigan ran for the cab.

Heard Roy yelling, Staggers yelling. Heard the booming explosion of the gunshot just before he reached the running board.

He lunged for the handbar, grabbed it, hauled himself up. And saw Staggers falling to the deck, blood on his chest, Jesus, and Maxon standing there with confusion and rage on his face, and Roy swinging around toward him, brandishing a damn .45 automatic.

Hannigan kept on moving, caught Roy's wrist with his right hand, slapped his left arm around the man's thick neck and jerked him up against his own body. Maxon yelled something; Roy made an enraged snorting sound and tried to get the gun up between them, tried to rupture Hannigan with a knee. Hannigan twisted, took the knee on his upper thigh, levered the two of them around into the gangway—but it was like trying to hold on to a maddened animal. He could feel his grip on the wrist slipping as Roy flailed wildly against him with arms, legs, body, still making that bullish snorting noise.

Then Maxon was there, trying to help, only Hannigan had his back to the cab, jammed together with the other man in the gangway, and Maxon couldn't reach around to get at Roy. He threw his weight against them anyway, and that pitched Hannigan off-balance into Roy, broke his holds on both wrist and neck.

And sent the two of them toppling forward out of the gangway.

The short stranger wrenched free in midair, and Hannigan landed on his right side on nothing but gravelly dirt, with enough impact to half-stun him for a second. He rolled over, came up to his knees gagging on smoke, shaking his head to clear it—and Roy had lost the gun in the fall, was crawling away from Hannigan toward where it lay, a few feet distant, next to one of the locomotive's big wheels. Nearby there were shouts, confused shuffling footfalls: the other men starting to crowd around.

But none of them was close enough to Roy to keep him from getting to the automatic, and Hannigan pushed off his knees in a flat, awkward dive, clawed at the man's trailing leg. Got his fingers on the pants cuff but couldn't hold on to the material when Roy kicked forward. By the time he folded himself back onto his knees, the short stranger had the gun, came around with it, aimed it at Hannigan's head. Hannigan saw the wide bore and the smoke-blurred face above it like a Hallowe'en mask—shapeless, grotesque—and had a subliminal thought that they were the last things he would ever see, and his body tensed to meet the bullet in one final lunge—

Something made a spitting sound, then another, behind him to the left. And there were two red-black blotches on the front of Roy's sweater, one above the other, near the heart.

The shouting and shuffling of the men stopped at once, as if they had all suddenly been frozen into a tableau. The short man jerked back and up on his knees; the wildness went out of his face, leaving a kind of amazed bewilderment. He made a grunting, choking sound, and the automatic dropped out of his hand, and he fell over on top of it and lay there unmoving.

Hannigan slid around on all fours.

The thin stranger was standing in a crouch twenty feet distant, apart from all the others, and in his hand was a gun with a short silencing tube screwed onto the barrel.

FORTY

Zacharias straightened up and retreated another couple of steps, moving the Woodsman quickly from side to side. But none of the men was making any kind of move in his direction. Some of them were bent over with spasms of coughing and the rest were looking nervously at him, at Tully lying by the locomotive, up at the one-legged guy leaning out of the cab. He could see that they wanted to move, all right, but not at him, not even away from his gun. They wanted to get into those coaches and the hell away from here.

That was what Zacharias wanted right now, too, and it was why he'd shot Tully. The son of a bitch had found out about the ordnance somehow and it had put him over the edge: he'd gotten that .45 out of one of the boxcars, climbed up into the engine and thrown down on the people in there—probably with the crazy idea of forcing them to uncouple the boxcars. And they hadn't stood still for it, would never have stood still for it. He'd briefly considered the possibility himself and rejected it right away, because gun or no gun, they'd have all panicked and rushed him and torn him apart.

When he'd heard the shot and then seen Tully and the red-haired guy come tumbling out, he'd known he had to take control of the situation before it got out of hand. Tully hadn't left him any choice. He'd blown their cover wide open. And he might have killed a couple of the men, and that would just as sure have turned them into a mob. It would have been his ass as well as Tully's, then.

He shouted at the one-legged guy, "Where's the engineer?"

"He's shot, damn you."

Somebody else said, "Jesus!" and it got even more tense around there.

"Dead?" Zacharias yelled at the gimp.

"No, but he's in bad shape."

"You know how to drive this train?"

"I know how to drive it, yeah. But I've got to have a fireman; I can't handle it by myself."

Zacharias started to tell him to pick somebody, changed his mind when he saw the way the redhead down on the ground was staring at him. Troublemaker, that one—the leader type, a thinker. Zacharias wanted him where he could keep an eye on him, and that had to be up in the cab because he wasn't going to ride in one of those coaches again; he couldn't afford to. He had to have control of the train, too, if he was going to find a way clear of these mountains when they got to Springwood. *If* they got to Springwood before that ordnance blew them all to hell.

He snapped at the redhead, "You—smart guy. You know how to be a fireman?"

The red-haired man stared at him through the curling smoke. Up in the cab the one-legged guy shouted, "Not him, I need somebody who—"

"Shut up!"

The redhead said tightly, "I can handle the job."

"Then it's yours. Couple of the rest of you men take the engineer out and back to a coach. Hurry it up—now!"

He'd let them go with no time to spare. Another few seconds out here and they'd have jumped him. As it was, they did exactly what he told them. Three guys pushed up into the cab and the rest broke for the coach cars. A few seconds later the three came down carrying the wounded and unconscious old man, took him uptrack after the others. Then the redhead climbed up to join the gimp.

Zacharias stayed where he was, fighting dizziness from the smoke in his lungs, looking from the engine back to the coaches. Tully had begun to twitch a little there on the ground— still alive. But he wasn't trying to get up, wasn't able to get up or use the automatic again. Zacharias didn't bother to finish him.

When the three men passed the engineer into the first coach, Zacharias jumped up onto the running board and pulled himself inside the cab. Stood with his back braced against the tender wall.

"All right, they're loaded in," he told the gimp. "Get this bastard moving."

FORTY-ONE

As soon as Tyrell and Bennett and Al Logan carried Ed Staggers out of the cab, Maxon concentrated on the gauges and controls and on the tree outside between the rails. There was no time now to think about the two strangers, or the shootings, or having Hannigan up here with him as fireman. Or the fact that it had been twelve years since he'd driven the old 0-6-0 switcher in the Eureka yards, and then only briefly, under his father's supervision. He'd do the job because it was all up to him now; they were all dependent on him alone. He felt a kind of a grim, muted excitement. It was fitting in a way, by God—meaningful compensation for the leg he'd lost, a chance to be more than a man again, a chance to be a savior.

The Baldwin was low on water, he saw, and the oil pressure was down and the boiler pressure was up. Worry about those things later. The steam was still up, that was what mattered now. The tree—how would Staggers have dealt with it? Eased up to it, nosed it off? No, too much danger of it falling back between the rails. Ed would have rammed it, and that's what he would do, too. Ram it hard, ram it again if he had to, keep right on going with the throttle notched open.

Maxon was tensed and ready when the lean stranger came into the cab and told him everybody was loaded in, get moving. And he acted instantly. He yanked the whistle three times, signaling for Linscott and Baker to release the rear brakes, then worked the air lever. The air pump hammered as it fought to release the clamped brake shoes. The second the hammering stopped, he sucked in a breath and gave her steam.

Exhaust churning, wheel flanges grinding on the rails, the Baldwin jerked forward. The pilot slammed hard against the bottom of the tree. That impact rocked them in a reverse motion that snapped Maxon's head back, almost knocked Hannigan and the stranger off their feet. Then there was the lunging impact of the tender and the other cars behind, and his head snapped forward again as the locomotive bucked the opposite way.

Outside, the tree skidded, teetered, started to slide back.

He threw the throttle open another notch, felt the power surge, and the pilot rammed the pine again—and this time, as it slid ahead, the charred, broken upper bole swung out at a forty-five-degree angle. They hit it a third time almost immediately, with less force; the pilot tapped it, locked against it, and the impetus of the straining engine shoved it all the way around like a swinging baseball bat and hurled it off the rails.

Free!

The Baldwin shuddered with the release of the tree's resisting weight, and soared ahead. The forward boxcar slapped against the tender again, making a booming metallic clatter. Then the string straightened out and their speed increased rapidly. Smoke shredded ahead of them, fanned out on both sides of the engine. The long white beam of the headlight probed through it and finally picked out the near half of the river trestle.

It was burning.

Maxon's heart stuttered; a laboring breath caught in his throat. Flames licked along the superstructure thirty feet below the tracks in one place out near the middle, and parallel to the tracks in another place closer in—but the fire had only just taken hold, hadn't started to race yet. There was still time; they could still get across.

But if those flames leaped up when they passed and torched off the wood sidings on one of the boxcars . . .

Frantically, Maxon gave her more steam. They would hit the trestle faster than was completely safe, but it was a risk he had to take. The fires on the bridge were a much greater threat. The headlamp illuminated more and more of the trestle as they bore down on it, along with upper sections of the river gorge's fern-coated far wall and the dense perimeter of the timberland through which the tracks ran beyond the river. Tattered wisps and patches of red-tinged smoke drifted like tule fog inside the gorge.

When the train sped out onto the trestle, the weakening superstructure seemed to shimmy with the vibrations from the tons of hurtling steel. The thunder of the wheels, the drivers, the turbine took on a hollow tone. Through the hanging smoke, Maxon got a fleeting impression of the narrow river gleaming blackly far below, but his attention was focused on the nearer spreading line of fire threatening the tracks ahead. The flames flickered erratically in the wind drafts, sending out sparks that caught on other parts of the trestle and set more of the wood frame to burning. Fire began to flank the rails on the southernmost third of the structure, creating a gauntlet for them to run before they could get clear of the bridge and into the timber.

Shaking, swaying, the engine reached the two-thirds point and nosed between the lengthening fire lines, through flames where they leaped up in the center ties in one place. Weird smoky shadows danced wildly through the cab.

Maxon saw fire surge upward close to his open side glass, heard the lean stranger shout something and move away to the middle of the footplate. Maxon swiveled his head long enough to see that the stranger still had his balance, was clinging to the tender bulkhead with his free hand. Then he jerked his gaze back to the burning tracks ahead.

Fifty yards to the end of the trestle.

Heat surrounded Maxon, so intense that his teeth ached. He could barely breathe; his mouth and throat were sand-dry. He hunched his shoulders, half-expecting the munitions to let go in an explosion he would never hear or feel.

Twenty-five yards.

And there wasn't any more fire in front of them, just the black ribbons of the tracks and the wilderness that walled the right-of-way on both sides.

The Baldwin clamored off the trestle, then the box-cars, then the coaches.

Made it, made it, made it.

Retching, Maxon put his head out through the side window to look back along the string. He couldn't see any fire on the boxcars on that side, or on the coaches, either. The streaming wind cleared his lungs momentarily, and he pulled his head back inside and swung it around to order Hannigan to check the left side of the train. But Hannigan was already at the gangway there, looking out and back, and a moment later he pivoted and called, "No fire on this side. What about yours?"

"Clear." Maxon squinted his stinging eyes, checked the steam gauge. Pressure dropping, down to one twenty. He felt a cut of anger through his relief and bellowed at Hannigan, "More coal! More coal, god-damn it, do your job if you know how!"

Hannigan gave him a quick, hard, unreadable look, turned immediately to pick up the shovel, pushed past the tight-faced stranger to lean inside the tender.

The heat had lessened considerably now that they were pulling well clear of the trestle, and the smoke in the cab had begun to dissipate. The air was almost breathable again without painful lung protest. Sweat started to flow on Maxon's body, plastering his clothes to his skin. He stared through the oblong front glass, saw the curve coming up ahead that would take them deep into unbroken timberland. Once they were through that, he thought, he would open her out and hope to God the water lasted for the remaining seven miles to Springwood.

On impulse, as they approached the curve, he craned out of the side window for another look behind them. Fire had claimed most of the trestle now; it was already sagging in the middle, was within minutes of burning collapse.

And the tops of the fir trees nearest the gorge on this side were just beginning to flame.

FORTY-TWO

Down on her knees between two of the coach seats, Regina stared at the gaping exit wound in Ed Staggers' shoulder and tried not to be sick. She had trained as a student nurse for a year before marrying Jim, but she had never gotten used to the sight of torn and bloody flesh, of human suffering, and she was sure she would have washed out eventually if she hadn't quit on her own.

She still didn't know what had happened to him. There'd been confusion and near-panic when they brought him into the car. Martha Staggers had gone into hysterics, flung herself on her husband as soon as he was laid on the seat, and it had taken Irv Norcross and Jack Bennett to pull her away. Women and children had cried frightened questions that were ignored because the men were shouting for all of them to hold on, there was a tree blocking the tracks and the locomotive was going to have to hit it and push it free, something Regina had already known because a couple of the women had gone outside to find out why they'd stopped.

Her own feeling of numbness had spread, kept her sitting where she was, while Jack and Al Logan used their hands and bodies to hold Ed on the seat as the train suddenly began to move. *But who's driving it?* she'd thought. *Jim? Is it Jim?* Then there'd been a series of awful rocking jolts, and they had begun moving faster; they'd gone out onto the river trestle. *Where's Steve? Why isn't Steve here?* And there had been flames shooting up around the car, cries, and then the flames were gone and the trestle was behind them, and it wasn't so terribly hot and smoky in there, and she remembered her nurse's training and managed to fight off some of the numbness and make herself stand and go to Ed's side.

He was unconscious and in shock, and his shirt was sodden with blood, so much blood, and his face was very pale. She'd checked his pulse, found it irregular but fairly strong. Then, with the help of Jack and Al, she'd gotten his shirt off and his head elevated and his body turned on his left side on the seat.

The bullet had exited cleanly enough, but God, the size of the wound! She bit her lip against the rise of nausea inside her, tore off part of her blouse and used the wadded-up piece to swab blood gingerly from the ragged hole. Coagulated blood: the wound wasn't bleeding any more. I can't do anything for him, she thought, what can I do for him without medical supplies? Just clean the wound as best she could, bandage it with more strips of clothing.

Al and Jack were kneeling on the next seat, bent forward over the back and holding Staggers' limp body for her. They both seemed relieved, almost drained by their safe passage across the trestle, as if that were an obstacle they had not believed could be overcome. Regina said to Logan, "Get me something to make bandages with, Al. Nothing with dirt on it—underclothes, a skirt."

He nodded, pushed away.

Sound washed over her as she worked: the roar of the train wheels, the moaning of Martha Staggers, the rise and fall of voices. She could make out words here, phrases there—enough to know that the men were explaining now what had happened, but not enough to make any sense of the story.

"Jack," she said to Bennett, "tell me how Ed got shot."

He hesitated. Then: "I'm not sure exactly. Way it looked, that fat stranger just went crazy and let him have it up in the locomotive cab."

"My God—you mean there's a crazy man up there—"

"No, no. That one's . . . dead now."

"Dead? What happened to him?"

Hesitation, longer this time.

"Jack? How did the stranger die?"

"The other one, his partner, killed him."

"Killed him," she said numbly. "How?"

"Shot him."

"With the same gun—?"

"No. Another one."

She shook her head, trying to understand.

Bennett said, "But nobody else was hurt."

"Why would they have guns?"

His eyes flicked. "I don't know."

"Who are they? *What* are they?"

"I don't know, Regina."

"Is the other stranger in the cab?"

"Yeah. But—"

"And Jim is driving the train, isn't he?"

A reluctant nod. "But he's okay, he—"

"Who took over as fireman?"

"Steve Hannigan."

She closed her eyes. When she opened them again after a moment, Bennett's drawn face swam before her, settled slowly back into focus. Both of them, she thought. Oh my God, *both* Jim and Steve up there with an armed man who murdered his own friend. Why? *Why?* There wasn't any sense to it, it was unreal, this whole night was unreal.

Bennett said, "Regina, you okay?"

She shook her head another time, only then it became a convulsive nod. The numbness had started to creep through her again as they talked, and now it had control of her mind. She felt faint; she wanted to lie down; she wanted to be sick. Instead she watched her hands, independent creatures, moving over Ed Staggers' naked back, against the bloody shoulder wound. There was blood on her fingers. Each of her fingers was stained and sticky with blood.

Logan came back to kneel beside her and begin silently to tear the articles of clothing he held into bandage-sized strips.

Regina watched his hands working, watched her own hands working.

Blood. And fire and guns and death.

Jim and Steve, Steve and Jim . . .

The train hurtled her onward through the dark mad night.

FORTY-THREE

In the swaying cab Hannigan stood tensely with one hip cocked against the fireman's seat, holding the fire shovel in both hands—not so much resting as waiting and worrying. He'd wanted to take an active and more direct role in matters, and now he had it, but he wished to Christ he didn't. He was doing the fireman's job well enough, that wasn't it. It was the shooting of

Staggers and Roy, and the lean stranger with his silenced gun. And the fact that Maxon now had control of the Baldwin, effective control of all their lives.

Maxon bothered him as much as any of the other things. The man seemed to know how to drive the old steamer, and yet he was handling her with a kind of heedless abandon. He had the throttle wide open, pushing the Baldwin to her limits, making her rock from side to side as if she were a steam-propelled cradle. The safety valves had begun to pop, and the beat of the turbine was irregular, laboring, like an old man's heart that was ready to give out. The manifold gauges, when Hannigan had looked at them moments ago, said that while the steam was up full, they had less than a quarter tank of water left and the boiler pressure was at four hundred pounds and climbing.

Damn it, there was no reason now for full speed and a full firebox. It was an unnecessary risk. The trestle was a good mile behind them, Springwood was only six miles down the line, and the fire was no longer an immediate threat—which meant that an explosion of the munitions in the boxcars was no longer an immediate threat, either. Except for the glare of the headlight and a faint high flush in the sky, they were surrounded by darkness; the air was tainted with the smell of smoke, but it was clear, you could breathe it now without difficulty. There wasn't any way the fire could catch them if they ran at two-thirds throttle; Maxon should know that even better than he did.

Abruptly Maxon shouted across to him, "Keep stoking, Hannigan! I want that box kept full."

"We don't need it full," Hannigan answered. "And we don't need a wide-open throttle either. Back off on the steam, let the boiler cool down a little—"

"Who the hell are you to tell me what to do?"

"Listen—"

"Not to you, homesteader. You wouldn't be here if it'd been up to me."

Hannigan's hands tightened around the shovel. He could feel the hatred well up inside him, tasted it like bile on the back of his tongue. And fought it down, controlled it. He was not a violent man, and violence inside him was unsettling. He'd been part of enough of it tonight, seen what it could do to other men. If he gave in to it inside himself, he would lose something of himself in the process: he would never be the same again.

He looked out nervously through the left-side window. Ahead, the tracks made a long gradual loop to the east, along the shore of a tiny mountain lake—one of dozens pocketed in glacial basins all through this wilderness. The water gleamed like oil; the evergreens tiered around it had a surreal appearance, like a Dali painting of spectators around a sports field. And above the trees to the east, he saw then, were the red and green running lights of a low-flying airplane. Another of the air tankers sent out to bomb the fire with chemicals.

It was at least two miles away when it drew abreast of the lake, but the pilot had to have seen them—the headlight, the smoke pouring out of the boiler stack. There wasn't anything he could do for them now except radio in to wherever he was based and let the Forestry officials know that the train was coming. The men on the fire lines that must have been set up both inside and outside Springwood by now would be alerted. Evacuation facilities would be waiting for them.

Slow down, Maxon, damn you. We're going to be all right.

But when Hannigan pulled his head back inside he heard Maxon shouting at him again, ordering him to stoke the firebox. Hannigan looked over at him, saw his face set in tight lines and his eyes hard and bright, and knew there was nothing to be gained in trying to argue with the man. Reluctantly, because he wasn't sure yet what he could do about Maxon's recklessness, he took the shovel back onto the footplate in front of the tender. He'd keep stoking for now, but he'd do it at his own pace and with light shovelfuls of coal.

As he came up to the tender, the stranger pivoted slightly against the right-hand bulkhead to watch him, as he'd done before. Hannigan hesitated, braced a shoulder against the left-side bulkhead.

On impulse he said to the lean man, "I want to ask you a question."

"No questions. Just keep working."

"This is important."

"Yeah?"

"What happens when we get to Springwood?"

"Nothing happens unless you make it happen."

"No more shooting?"

"I told you, that's up to you. All I'm interested in is saving my ass, same as the rest of you."

Hannigan had been watching the man's face, his eyes, in the spill of light from the cab lamp. The features were set hard, with a different kind of hardness from that in Maxon's face, like something made of stone. The eyes seemed lidless and they didn't blink: a lizard's eyes. Dangerous, amoral. But he was also in full control of himself. He wouldn't kill anybody else unless he was forced to; Hannigan believed him about that. The only thing he and Maxon had to worry about was the way things looked when they reached both the fire lines and Springwood. If the stranger could get away on his own, by jumping out of the cab while they were still moving, he'd do it that way. If the odds were stacked against him, he'd take one of them hostage.

Maxon or me, he thought ironically. Rivals here, too. Which one of us for the hostage? Which one of us for Regina?

"Hannigan!"

Maxon's voice again. Hannigan looked over, saw him swing half around on the high seat, and thought he was going to continue shouting for more coal.

Instead Maxon said, "Come over here a minute."

Hannigan frowned, glanced at the stranger, got nothing in return, and crossed to stand beside Maxon. "What is it?"

"Look at this," Maxon said loudly, and pointed down to where the reverse lever was. Hannigan looked, didn't see anything, but Maxon bent down close beside him and said, "Time to see what you're made of, Hannigan," in a lowered voice that couldn't carry above the boiler noise.

"What?"

"We've got to get that bastard's gun," Maxon said, and there was both urgency and guile in his tone now. "No telling what he might do when we get near Springwood."

"He's not going to do anything—"

"We can't take that chance. Go back over there, keep him talking. And hang on to something. I'm going to shut down the steam and throw the air open enough to buck us and pitch him off-balance. You grab his gun, heave him out the gangway if you can do it."

176

Hannigan stared at him. "Jesus," he said, "you want to get us both killed?"

"He won't know it's coming."

"He's not stupid and he's on his guard. It's too much of a risk. He won't shoot either of us if we—"

"You going to help me?"

"No. For Christ's sake, man, we're out of fire danger now; we're going be okay. Use your head."

Maxon's face turned blood-dark with rage. "You goddamn coward!"

Hannigan felt the hatred surge inside him, wanted to grab Maxon by the neck and shake him—and behind them the lean one yelled suddenly, "That's enough talking! Get the hell away from each other!"

The words jerked Hannigan erect, made him back off a step. The stranger had come forward and was standing with his feet spread wide apart, right hand anchored against the cab bulkhead, left hand holding the gun steady. His expression hadn't changed any, but there was cold, deadly menace in his eyes. He was not a man you could overpower, like the short one had been; he was not a man you could fool. No matter what the circumstances, you would never, never catch him unawares.

Hannigan put his gaze back on Maxon, and the booming purr of the wheels seemed to magnify in his ears, a wad of ice seemed lodged in his chest. The rage was gone from Maxon's face; it was as expressionless as the lean man's. But his eyes now were stubborn and determined; his eyes said it all.

He's going to try it anyway, Hannigan thought. With or without my help, he's going to go after that gun.

FORTY-FOUR

Blind with pain, Tully crawled around in the dirt and gravel beside the tracks, trying to find enough strength to lift his body onto his knees. Heat assaulted him in pulsing waves. Smoke filled his lungs and he couldn't breathe. Inside his head there was a grayness like the smoke, swirling; in his ears a crackling roar grew and grew until it was a shattering pressure against his eardrums. He didn't know how long it had been since Zacharias had shot him; he'd slipped in and out of consciousness once, twice, half a dozen times. Didn't know anything at all except terror.

The fire, the fire.

No!

The *fire*—

Something hot fell on his back, burned him, and he made a mewling noise that became a choking gasp as he twisted violently on the ground. His body flopped, twisted again, and he found himself on his knees. He dragged his arms up and dug fingers into his eyes, gouged them open. Grayness. And light—flames. All around him, everywhere, reaching out for him.

No!

And the tracks—empty, empty; the train was gone.

He lunged upward on legs that seemed like jelly, reeled, and fell down again. Burst of agony in his chest, blood in his mouth. A flaming cinder winked out of the grayness and hit him on the arm. He recoiled, beat off the cinder, vomited a thin streamer of blood, and lunged to his feet again.

No!

He stumbled forward, fell, got up, fell, got up. Black seeped in around the swirling gray at the edges of his mind. Yellow-red light bloomed massively ahead of him through the smoke, brightened, and he saw the trestle, and the light became a line of grasping fire as high as a building—it was all over the trestle, eating it, killing it, turning it black and shapeless and making it groan and shriek and begin to crumble.

Fire fire fire fire fire—

And a tree limb, a burning tree limb, fell out of the smoke and hit him a glancing blow across the back.

And set his sweater ablaze.

He went blind again with agony, spun around and around in circles like a mad dog chasing its tail. Couldn't reach the fire, and stopped spinning and ripped at the sweater, tried to pull it over his head, did pull it off and hurled it away. Only by then the flames had found his pants, leaped up to feed on his hair, clawed at his naked back. It had him, *it had him!*

He screamed.

His father screamed.

Tully and his father ran screaming out of the burning house and up between the railroad tracks, on fire, beating at the clinging flames.

Tully and his father fell into the street and onto the ties and lay there writhing, shrieking Help me! Help me!

Tully and his father.

Dying.

FORTY-FIVE

Maxon waited until the Baldwin neared the long eastward loop around the lake's south shore before he got ready to make his move.

He had his left hand tight on the throttle, and he moved his right over and let it rest on the air-brake lever. Then he eased around slowly on the seat, planted his left foot on the footboard, slid the artificial leg out from under the reverse bar. Hannigan, the gutless bastard, was backed up against the fireman's seat, watching him with a tense, nervous expression on his face. The hell with you, Maxon thought, and looked at the stranger. That one was watching him too, impassively, his body again wedged flat against the bulkhead. The silenced automatic was steady in his hand.

The man had to be disarmed or thrown out of the cab, that was all there was to it. Maxon had known that as soon as he'd had time to think about the situation after they pulled away from the trestle. The stranger was a cold-blooded killer, and maybe even worse than that, because he was obviously mixed up somehow with what was in those boxcars. The way he'd murdered his partner, just shot him like he was a tin target—that kind of person was capable of doing anything to save himself. Capable of shooting both him and Hannigan once they got near Springwood, locking the throttle open, and then jumping clear: creating a runaway that would eventually crash, just so he could get away in the confusion. Hannigan, because he was a coward, didn't want to think anybody would do an inhuman thing like that. But Maxon knew better. Making a move against the stranger was risky, but it was a hell of a lot less risky than doing nothing at all.

Determination mingled with Maxon's rage, heightened the feeling of excitement he'd had ever since taking control of the throttle. All up to him— this part of it, too. And he'd be equal to it, just as he'd been equal to everything else tonight.

He inclined his body back to peer out again through the side window. Ahead, the twin black rails were beginning to curve beyond the reach of the headlight; in another few seconds the Baldwin would lean swaying into the turn. When he braked, the jolt would sharpen the listing angle, and maybe that in itself would be enough not only to knock the stranger off-balance but to spill him right out of the gangway. Small chance, but he had to take advantage of every possibility.

His teeth clamped together and he set himself. The locomotive started into the curve with a small lurching shock—

And Hannigan suddenly pushed away from the fireman's seat and barked at him, "Maxon, for God's sake don't do it!"

A kind of frenzy came into Maxon—*you son of a bitch!*—and he braced himself on the seat, shut the throttle, and hit the air.

There was a moment of headlong drifting motion. Then the brake shoes began to lock and grind and the Baldwin jarred, pulled back, shuddered forward again when the tender plowed into it from behind. Hannigan was thrown along the far side of the boiler and into the piping on the front bulkhead. The stranger lost his grip on the tender bulkhead, came staggering away from it. His free hand groped out to the gangway

181

jamb behind Maxon, his knees bent and his feet sliding wider apart as he fought to hold his balance.

Maxon was already moving by then. He came off the seat on his good left foot, twisted his body around, and slapped his left hand against the side bulkhead at the same time his aluminum foot came down on the deck. That held him steady long enough to swing forward again and roll his weight back onto his left foot. He came right up to the stranger, half-turned away from him at the gangway frame. Reached out for him, dug his left hand into the man's shoulder and threw his right against the nearest hip: *shove him through the gangway, shove him off the train.* For an instant he thought he had enough leverage to do it—

Only then the stranger got his body braced and lunged back into him, brought his right elbow and forearm around in a vicious backhand sweep. Maxon saw it coming, tried to dodge, but his goddamn artificial foot slipped on the deck—and the blow hit him full force, forearm thudding into his chin and the right side of his face, elbow cracking against his collarbone. His head snapped back and to the left; there was a flash of light and pain behind his eyes. The stranger came all the way around in front of him then, savagery in his face, and swung the gun up over his head. And kicked the aluminum leg out from under him.

Maxon went down. The silencer on the gun glanced across the side of his head as he fell, struck him again, more solidly, when he landed asprawl on his buttocks.

The wail of the brake shoes quit in that moment, then the bucking motion of the cab ceased. The string smoothed out, the train began to pull ahead at a retarded speed through the curve and onto another tangent. Pain blurred Maxon's vision, blurred his mind, but the frenzy wouldn't let him give up. He dragged himself up onto his left knee, tried to stand again.

The stranger kicked him in the stomach.

All the air went out of him, all his strength, too, and he toppled over backward against the footboard and lay there gasping, hurting. Dimly he saw Hannigan standing above him at the controls—he'd shut off the air and opened the throttle halfway—and the lean man bent forward in front of him, breathing hard through his mouth, pointing the fat muzzle of the silencer at Maxon's right eye.

"You try anything else," the stranger shouted, "I'll blow your fucking head off! You understand me? I'll blow your fucking head right off!"

Seconds passed with all three of them frozen in position. Then the lean man straightened, backed off slowly to the tender. Maxon's smoke-weakened lungs finally dragged in enough air to let him breathe again without panting. Some of the terrible pain in his head and stomach eased, and his vision and his thoughts cleared. There was oozing wetness on his right temple. He put a hand up there and then took it down and looked at a smear of blood.

"Get up," the stranger told him. The savagery had gone out of his face, left it impassive again. "Get back on your seat."

Maxon laid a hand on the footboard, lifted himself onto it. Hannigan reached down to help him, but Maxon slapped wrathfully at the hand and said, "Get away from me, you cocksucker," through clamped teeth. His voice sounded as if it were full of liquid. He pushed off the footboard, caught the seat and hauled himself erect. And threw a hard deliberate shoulder into Hannigan that sent him reeling out of the way.

Hannigan caught his balance, took a step back toward him, hesitated, and then retreated to the fireman's seat. His eyes were angry, his mouth thinned down to a slash.

Looking at him, Maxon felt heat rise in his face—a combination of fury and hatred and frustration. Hannigan's fault, damn him to hell. If he'd cooperated in the beginning, they wouldn't still be under the gun. Even if he'd just kept his mouth shut instead of shouting the way he had, putting the stranger on his guard, the lean man would be long gone out the gangway. Lousy son of a bitch coward! If they got out of this in spite of Hannigan, he'd fix him. One way or another he'd fix him good.

Maxon slid up onto the seat, wiped blood and sweat from his face with shaking fingers, and squinted at the gauges. Goddamn steam pressure was down under a hundred pounds. He caught the throttle, notched it wide open again. The Baldwin surged, smoke peppered with cinders poured out of the barking stack, the beat of the wheels and drivers again built up to a thunderous cadence. The oil pressure was still down, too; he opened the lubricator nozzle all the way. Then he glanced around at Hannigan.

"More coal!" he bellowed. "Load up full."

Hannigan didn't move.

"More coal, I said. I want that box full."

"Damn it," Hannigan said, "we're less than five miles out of Springwood, maybe no more than three from the fire lines—"

"I'm the engineer here; I know what I'm doing. You don't. Load that box!"

Behind him the stranger said to Hannigan, "Do what he says."

"Listen—"

"You heard me."

Hannigan's hands were drawn into white-knuckled fists. But he didn't argue any more. He turned and grabbed up the shovel and headed back onto the footplate.

All right, Maxon thought blackly. He put his head out the side window to look uptrack. The fire was a good mile behind them now; the smoky glow seemed to coat the whole of the northern sky. He swung his gaze downtrack. More dense timberland here, the right-of-way walled on both sides by virgin spruce and Douglas fir. The tracks ran straight for another mile, finally came out of the heavy forest in front of an eroded-granite escarpment and then hooked sharply around it to the west. All right. The stranger wouldn't be expecting him to try the same thing twice, or to try anything so soon after the first attempt, so that was when and where he'd make his second move. Right there on the curve, when the Baldwin leaned into it.

Hannigan had made him fail once, but that hadn't changed anything. He still knew what he had to do.

And this time, by God, *nothing* would stop him from doing it.

FORTY-SIX

Warily, Zacharias watched the redhead shovel coal into the firebox and the one-legged guy hunch forward at the controls. Particularly the one-legged guy.

He'd known something was in the wind ever since the two of them had their heads together, talking in low-pitched voices so he couldn't hear them. But he'd been paying more attention to the redhead, and that was why the gimp had almost been able to push him out of the cab right after his bright idea of putting the brakes on. Well, he wouldn't make that mistake twice. The redhead might be a thinker and a leader, but he had sense, he'd kept his cool. The other one was a hothead, big hero type, plenty of guts but shit for brains. Zacharias should have seen that right away, would have if he'd been in any other kind of situation, any other kind of place than the cab of a steam locomotive that was trying to outrace a forest fire.

You could just see that one sitting over there now trying to figure out some other stupid trick. Sooner or later he'd come up with something, and then he'd try it. And when he did? Zacharias didn't want to have to put his lights out because he wasn't sure the redhead could operate the train. That was all that had kept him from shooting the gimp a couple of minutes ago. But if the one-legged guy's next bright idea couldn't be dealt with easily, he'd have to waste him, all right, and take his chances with the redhead. They'd been damn lucky so far to get clear of the fire without the ordnance in those boxcars blowing up. He wasn't about to let a macho gimp push him right out of luck.

Luck. Yeah.

His own chances weren't any too good as it was, no use kidding himself. He still had to get away from the train either before or after they reached Springwood, and to safe ground after that. And there'd be cops all over the place, that was for sure. There were always plenty of cops in a disaster area. So he couldn't be in this cab when the train stopped—unless they could go all the way *through* Springwood, stop somewhere past the town where there weren't any people waiting. But that figured to be a long shot.

Or did it?

The redhead was coming to the tender again for more coal. Zacharias said to him, "These tracks go all the way through Springwood?"

The question got him a frown and a look before the redhead said, "Through Springwood?"

"That's right—through it and out the other side."

"Not exactly."

"What's that mean?"

"There are tracks leading out of the Springwood yards, but not the ones we're on. This is an old spur line."

"They don't connect?"

"They connect through a series of switches. But if you're thinking of having us go right through the yards onto one of the other lines, it won't work. Half of those switches will be closed, and there's liable to be cars or switch engines blocking some of the others."

Zacharias didn't think the redhead was lying to him; it sounded reasonable. Scratch that idea. He said, "Okay, smart guy, get back to your shoveling." Then, because the gimp was looking around at him, "You—put those eyes up front."

Both of them did as they were told.

He ran his tongue over dry, ashy lips. So he was left with two choices, as far as he could see now. One: ride into the town, take one of these guys as hostage—the redhead; the gimp would be trouble, if he wasn't already dead—and grab a car and order the law not to follow. But he didn't like that worth a damn. The odds were too long. A gunman with a hostage would be about as important to the cops as the fire back there. They'd be on their radios the minute he was gone; they'd order surveillance if not roadblocks; he'd have to run for it with the law tight on his ass all the way. Two: jump clear before the train reached Springwood, at the fire lines the redhead had talked about a couple of minutes ago, and lose himself in the woods and try to find a car somewhere he could steal. That made more sense. And it was probably what he'd wind up doing, because it would buy him a little time. There'd be confusion when the train stopped, and it would take the cops a while to sort out the story about him. And even when they did they'd be inclined to pay more attention to evacuating people, to the oncoming fire, than to one man running around loose somewhere in the area. They'd put out an alert on him, sure, but it wouldn't be the same kind of manhunt as if he took a hostage. If his luck kept on holding he'd be out of the area long before they could mobilize against him.

The one-legged guy had his head cocked around again, looking at Zacharias with one narrowed eye. Zacharias didn't say anything this time, just stared back at him. Almost immediately the gimp shifted his gaze and yelled to the redhead to hurry it up, quit dogging it, get the goddamn firebox loaded. The redhead ignored him. He was leaning forward in front of the boiler, peering at one of the gauges there.

Something between the two of them, Zacharias thought. They seemed to have hard-ons for each other, the gimp in particular for the redhead, and it wasn't just what had been happening here in the cab. But that was good—it helped keep them from allying themselves against him. When the gimp made his next stupid move, as it looked like he might pretty soon, he'd be making it alone again.

Zacharias flexed his finger against the Woodsman's trigger.

Waiting.

FORTY-SEVEN

When Hannigan released the foot pedal to reclose the firebox doors against the white glare and the blast of heat from within, he backed over to the fireman's seat instead of going back to the tender for more coal. He just couldn't keep on feeding the ballast any longer. The safety valves were popping steadily now, like strings of firecrackers going off, and the needle on the boiler-pressure gauge hovered near six hundred pounds. She was badly overheated; the relief valves couldn't handle that kind of pressure indefinitely.

Maxon should have known that, too, but he wasn't paying any attention to the gauges or to the sounds of the valves. He was just sitting over there with his face closed tight, his eyes reflecting a kind of obsessive intensity, shouting at intervals for more coal. He'd let his emotions and his role in this tragedy blind him, rob him of all perspective. He wasn't about to listen to anybody but himself, and what he was hearing inside his own head were distortions and fallacies: disarming or jettisoning the stranger, maintaining maximum speed all the way to the end of the line.

Pretty soon the damn fool was going to make his second try at the lean man—it was so plain in his face and his movements that he might as well have been wearing a sign. And if Hannigan knew it, the stranger had to know it, too. Whatever else the man was, he was also sharp-witted and alert. The way he'd handled Maxon a few minutes ago proved that. He hadn't lost control of the situation for more than a second or two. Hannigan had seen that immediately after regaining his equilibrium in the jouncing cab, which was why he had gone straight to the controls instead of trying to help Maxon. If he had interfered, either he or Maxon would be dead now—there wasn't any doubt of that in his mind.

Sweat streamed from his armpits, rolled down over his naked sides. He still wasn't sure what to do. Maybe he shouldn't do anything at all. Maybe it would be best for everyone on this train if Maxon just went ahead and made another move and the stranger shot him dead. That would solve the problem of the overheating boiler well enough.

Solve the problem of which of us gets Regina, too.

Christ! What kind of thinking was that? Fatigue and frustration and the constant level of tension corrupting his mind. Peripherally he was aware that the sky to the east was turning a dim lavender-gray, that the edges of the heavy darkness that surrounded them were beginning to smooth off. Dawn just a few minutes away now. Twenty-four hours since he had last slept. His body ached, his head ached, his muscles felt atrophied; for all its negative effects, the tension, like an adhesive, was all that was holding him together.

What if he went over and hit Maxon, knocked him out, and then took over the throttle himself? But he'd never driven a locomotive in his life; there were too many things he didn't know about its practical operation. And he might not even be able to knock Maxon out in the first place. For one thing, the man was strong, full of cunning and resolution. For another, the stranger might decide to spare Maxon because he was the one driving the train, and shoot *him* for making the attack.

The feeling of helplessness came into him again. Damn it, he had to do something—he *had* to. Take on Maxon anyway? Appeal to him again? Appeal to the stranger about the boiler threat?

"More coal, damn you!" Maxon yelled at him again.

Hannigan moved then, compulsively. Went around the boiler to stand a couple of paces away from Maxon on the high seat. "No more coal," he said angrily. "We're almost out of water, for God's sake. Look at the pressure gauge: the boiler's too hot already."

"The hell it is."

"The hell it isn't. Listen to those safety valves, man. *Listen* to them."

"You listen to them while you're stoking."

"I'm telling you, she's liable to blow!"

"Bullshit."

"Goddamn it," Hannigan said, "it's only four miles to Springwood, maybe half that to where the fire lines should be—"

From over by the tender the stranger shouted, "What the hell're you two arguing about? What's the matter?"

Hannigan looked at him. "The boiler's overheated," he answered. "If we don't slow down, relieve some of the pressure before we run out of water, it could explode."

The man scowled. "What about that?" he demanded of Maxon.

"He doesn't know what he's talking about. He doesn't know anything about steam locomotives; he's a lousy book writer."

"I mean it!" Hannigan yelled. "It could explode!"

There was indecision in the stranger's face; he didn't know which of them to listen to. He asked Maxon, "You sure he's not right about that boiler?"

"Damn right I'm sure."

Hannigan shouted, "Come over here and take a look at the boiler gauge yourself! You'll see I'm telling the truth."

The lean man didn't move. "The hell with that. I wouldn't know what I was seeing."

"The needle's in the danger zone, you can tell that much."

"Sure she's running hot," Maxon said, "but that doesn't mean anything. Not yet it doesn't. If she runs too hot I'll shut her down. Right now we need full power; we can't afford to cut speed. Look outside, you'll see how close that fire is behind us."

The stranger still didn't move. But the indecision vanished, and as Hannigan had feared he would, he said, "All right then. The quicker we get where we're going, the better." To Hannigan he said, "Get back over here and start shoveling. We'll keep things the way they are for the time being."

Frustration and pent-up rage had swelled the cords in Hannigan's neck. "The time being might be all the time we've got left!"

"That's enough out of you, smart guy. Get to work."

Hannigan hesitated—but there wasn't anything more he could say that would change the man's mind. The racing fire and the urgent need for escape were of greater concern to the stranger than a layman's analysis of a steam boiler he himself knew nothing about. Damn Maxon! How could he believe what he'd been saying? Even with his emotions running wild, he ought to have an idea of the danger.

Unless—

Unless he *was* aware of the danger, all right, but only intended to maintain full speed for a short while. Unless he was lying with a kind of heavy-handed cunning, because a wide-open throttle was part of another reckless scheme to attack the stranger.

Nails digging into his palms, Hannigan turned away from the boiler. Through the front window he saw that they were just emerging from the expanse of timberland. Ahead was a wide granite escarpment around which the tracks curved to the west—a plum-colored mass in the early-morning gloom. Four miles exactly from there to Springwood; he remembered Ed Staggers pointing the landmark out to him once on a railroad map in the Logspur roundhouse.

When he looked down at the boiler-pressure gauge he saw that the needle now was beyond the six-hundred-pound line.

He backed over to one of the side toolboxes, where he'd laid the shovel. Picked it up and stood there with it, trying to think, trying to decide what to do. Wait it out, let Maxon make his foolish move, hope it got him beaten or even shot? No good. The boiler could blow before he made the move; Hannigan could hear the popping of the valves growing louder by the second. Or Maxon could try it and get not only himself shot but Hannigan too. Something like that could happen easily enough in a confined space like this cab. If both of them went down, the train would become a runaway.

"Load up!" Maxon hollered at him. "Give me steam!"

Hannigan stared at the blackened shovel in his hands—the heavy square-sided shovel. Glanced across at Maxon again. And knew he had only one choice, that he had to act on it before it was too late.

Not just for the three of them—too late for everyone on this train.

Because if the boiler blew, the munitions in the boxcars would blow, too.

FORTY-EIGHT

Eyes narrowed, nostrils flared, Maxon watched the eroded rock escarpment loom closer beyond the Baldwin's headlight beam. In another minute they would be into the short westward curve, listing into a turn that was even sharper than the one back around the lake.

Another minute, just one more minute.

He leaned sideways around the throttle bar to look at the boiler gauge. Six hundred pounds, and climbing slowly. That gutless Hannigan was right about the boiler—but not as right as he thought. Old as she was, she could stand more than seven hundred pounds without blowing. A boiler like this wouldn't erupt until the pressure reached four times the working steam pressure; he knew that well enough, he'd had talks with his father and Ben Kiley about these old steamers: there wasn't any real danger yet. Long before she got near eight hundred pounds of pressure, he'd have shut her down and hit the air. And when he had the stranger's gun, when that bastard was down and out or gone through the gangway, he'd keep the Baldwin at one-third throttle the rest of the way in. Would have had to do that anyway because they were almost out of water: the water glass had already told him that.

Less than a minute now. Forty-five seconds.

Get the gun and lose the stranger, take the train safely across the fire lines and into Springwood—his responsibility, *his*. One-legged savior, by Christ. They'd never pity him again after tonight. Nobody would ever pity him again.

Thirty seconds.

Twenty.

The escarpment grew, jumbled rock jutting up to block off part of the purple-black sky. Curve three hundred yards distant, flanked by the cliff and by a long grassy slope that fell away to timber, to a dry stream bed thick with brush.

Fifteen seconds.

Maxon slid his buttocks around on the seat, put his right hand on the air-brake lever. Worked the aluminum leg into position. Boiler heat shimmied in the air, gave the interior of the cab a faintly distorted look. The engine groaned and shrieked as if it were in pain; the pounding rhythm of steel and steam was like a battle hymn in his ears.

Ten seconds.

And he saw Hannigan standing across from him with the shovel—just standing there with it up in front of his body like a rifle at port arms. Something in his face touched off an alarm signal in Maxon's brain.

Five seconds.

Hannigan took a fast, hard step toward him, and there was menace in the way he moved, menace in his eyes. *He's coming after me with that shovel!* The realization unleashed a flood of blind fury. In self-defense Maxon came up off the seat, let go of the throttle and air lever, pushed off the footboard. The stranger bellowed something behind him; he saw Hannigan jerk the shovel up and ducked instinctively, left hand coming up to protect his face, right hand starting a roundhouse swing at Hannigan's head—

There was a tremendous screaming, crunching noise. And the right side of the cab shattered like an eggshell.

Upheaval, sudden chaos. The locomotive wrenched violently, lifted, fell back; glass shattered, wood splintered, metal tore apart; shards and shrapnel flew through the cab. Maxon was hurled into Hannigan, and the two of them spun in a tangle of arms and legs, hit the fireman's seat and burst apart. Maxon caromed into the firebox shield, striking the lubricator on the boiler butt; it burst, sprayed him with hot oil. He came off in a sideways stagger, and through a dizzying oil-streaked blur he saw a huge spear of metal slash for an instant across the cab, miss him by a foot, and hurtle out through what was left of the front window panel.

A rod, Jesus, side rod let go—

Just as the awful understanding broke in on him that this was his fault, that he wasn't a savior at all, something struck him a vicious blow across the back of the head and knocked him senseless.

FORTY-NINE

Zacharias thought the boiler had blown up.

The wrenching of the cab ripped him loose of the tender bulkhead, threw him to the floor with pieces of glass and wood and metal raining down all around him, and in that moment he had a confused memory of the redhead shouting about the boiler, wanting to convince him it was too hot and might explode. Fear spiraled through him, clawed like a hand at his groin. The ordnance, it would blow, too—get out of here, jump, jump!

He twisted around on the heaving deck, got his left arm up over his head; he was still holding the Woodsman clenched in his right. There was a gaping hole in the right side of the cab, wind gusting in through it. Things had stopped flying around inside, and he had a glimpse of the one-legged guy lying sprawled out on his face with blood on his head, the redhead up on his feet and lunging toward the controls. Then Zacharias was up on knees and elbows, crawling frantically through broken glass that gouged at his body, cut his wrist, trying to get to the gangway.

But he didn't make it.

From down on the rails came the wailing screech of brake shoes locking, sparks flying up; the engine seemed to buckle for an instant, then careened wildly again and began to lose speed. The motion flung him away from the gangway, skidded him backward across the footplate and up against the tender. Coal bounced out of it, beat at him like hailstones. There was a surging impact behind them, and the locomotive lifted again, lost more speed as it fell back, lifted a third time.

Impact, even more violent.

A tearing-metal sound somewhere else on the train.

The engine wrenched sideways; the left side seemed to come right up off the rails. The redhead ran away from the controls—involuntarily, legs pumping in a crazy comic way—and the gimp's body and his own slid and tumbled that same direction. Zacharias felt himself jar into the bulkhead beside the left-hand gangway, felt the locomotive and the tender spin around to the left, coming off the tracks, and then tilt and jerk farther onto that side, as if they were being flipped around and over by another toppling weight behind them.

More metal ripped apart somewhere; the engine kept falling and sliding sideways across the rails.

The last thing Zacharias heard, before he was pulled free of the bulkhead, before he went spinning into darkness, was a series of echoing crashes that went on and on and on. . . .

FIFTY

Hannigan had been thrown clear.

One second he was desperately hanging on to the throttle in the pitching cab, and the next he was being propelled away, and after that he was through the gangway and airborne, weightless, dropping down through clouds of hissing steam. He landed on his feet on the slope that bordered the east side of the right-of-way, went down instantly with pain slashing through both legs, and rolled and kept on rolling pell-mell over dry grass and through brush. Barreled finally into the brittle remains of a dead tree that crumbled but broke his momentum, kicked him over on his back. He slid downward another couple of yards, feet first, then managed to dig hands and shoe heels into the turf and stop himself at the edge of a dry creek.

The terrible sounds of rent metal filled the dawn above him. He flopped onto his stomach, stunned and dizzy, and got up on one knee and shook his head until his eyes focused and he could see what was happening up there.

The two coach cars were still on the track, still safe—that was the first thing that registered on his mind.

They were past him by fifty yards, deeper into the curve around the granite escarpment, coasting to a stop, still coupled to the aft boxcar. Beyond them by another fifty yards, the forward boxcar had snapped loose from its couplers both fore and aft and had de-railed; it was lying angled and broken on its side on the grassy slope. Its doors had burst open and there were crates and boxes of weapons and ammunition strewn all over the slope, some of them still rolling, bouncing, splitting apart and spilling out more mu-nitions. And another thirty yards beyond the boxcar, partially obscured by the curve, the old Baldwin—headlight still burning—and its tender were just skidding to a stop, diagonally across the tracks, the locomotive upended half on its top like a dying giant beetle.

Hannigan pushed up onto his feet. There was agony in his legs, pain all through him, but he hadn't broken anything in the fall. He was able to move, even to run awkwardly up the slope at a forty-five-degree angle. The sounds of the crash were fading now as the Baldwin and the last of the rolling crates came to rest, and he could hear the cries and shouts of the people inside the coaches. He saw Joe Linscott and Sam Baker swing down from the rear platform of the caboose car, moving dazedly, Baker clutching at his right leg. None of the others had come out yet, but there was confused shadowy movement beyond the dark windows.

Regina, he thought. Regina.

Three-quarters of the way up the slope he started to turn toward the forward coach. Changed his mind, grimacing, and kept running along the slope past the cars, because there were the shattered locmotive and Maxon and the stranger to worry about, too. He wouldn't accomplish anything by trying to fight his way into the car to Regina; he would only add to the confusion.

As he neared the broken boxcar, the whole slope ahead of him looked like an abandoned battlefield. Handguns, carbines, submachine guns, grenade launchers, 7.62 millimeter and .30 and .45 and .50 caliber heavy machine guns; clips and boxes and belts and drums of ammunition—all gleaming blackly, evilly amid splintered wood and clumps of dry grass and brush. He scanned the area for Maxon and the stranger, didn't see any sign of either of them. Looked away and ran around the boxcar, coming up onto the right-of-way, and went down the loosened ties between bent and bowed steel rails.

Steam wafted all around the Baldwin and the tender, seemed to cling to the metal surfaces like marsh gas, and gave them an unearthly look in the gray half-light. Torn metal made little crackling noises; the boiler valves were still popping, but more faintly as the heat diminished, and Hannigan knew there wasn't any more danger of it exploding. Except for those sounds and the cries of the townspeople behind him, the wilderness surrounding the tracks was wrapped now in early morning stillness.

He looked up at the gaping hole in the right side of the cab. A side rod had let go, probably as a result of a broken crankpin, and it had sliced off the feed water pumps, air pump, running board—everything on that side—before slashing through the bulkhead. A miracle it hadn't decapitated one of the three of them when it ripped into the cab.

There were more sounds behind him, drawing near, but Hannigan paid no attention to them. He climbed up over the undercarriage, caught h)ld of the gangway frame, and hauled himself up .o where he could see inside. At first he thought .ne cab was empty; then, when he leaned in a little farther, he saw an arm and a leg, part of a body wedged down between the fireman's seat and the boiler and up against the front bulkhead.

Maxon.

Hannigan pulled himself into the cab, eased his body down along the canted deck until he was standing on the left-side bulkhead. He squatted there and took a close look at Maxon. Still alive: his chest was moving, his breath made a faint rasp through bloody nostrils. There was blood all over his head, a pulpy-looking area on the back of the skull—Hannigan

201

remembered seeing him hit by a piece of flying woodwork, stepping over the fallen body to get at the throttle and the emergency air. Maxon's artificial leg was gone, torn loose in the crash; his right pants leg was crumpled under the leg stump.

Hannigan probed quickly at the inert form, didn't find any broken bones. Then he got a two-handed grip under Maxon's arms and tugged until he was able to prop him face down against the deck, with his head up toward the gangway.

Outside there were running footsteps, voices. Somebody said, "Christ, a rod must've let loose, that's what happened," and somebody else shouted, "Hannigan! You need help in there?"

"Yeah—I've got Maxon."

There were scraping sounds on the undercarriage, and a moment later Joe Linscott's face appeared in the gangway. He scrambled inside the cab, dropped down beside Hannigan, and Lloyd Tyrell came up to take his place in the opening.

Looking at Maxon, Linscott said, "How bad is he?"

"Alive."

"Where's the one with the gun?"

"I don't know. He must've been thrown out after I was."

"I hope he wasn't as lucky as you," Linscott said grimly.

Hannigan peered up at Tyrell. "Anybody hurt in the cars?" he asked.

"Few people bruised up," Tyrell told him, "and Jack Bennett's daughter's got a busted arm."

Regina's all right, then. She's all right.

Weakened muscles straining, Hannigan helped Linscott lift the unconscious man up to where Tyrell could get a hold on him. Among the three of them, then, they got Maxon out of the cab, and two of the other men who had reached the locomotive lowered him to the ground outside. Hannigan climbed out painfully, ahead of Linscott, went down the under-carriage. Uptrack he saw that everyone was out of the coaches now, running and stumbling toward the engine in a ragged line. At the rear of the line Logan and Lee Adcock were carrying Staggers—and near the front, her face a mask of worry and fright, was Regina.

But Hannigan stared past her, not at her, and a cop-pery taste came into his mouth.

Because what he was looking at was the reddish glow in the sky to the north, paler now as the darkness grayed steadily with dawn light, but high and smoke-crowned. And he was feeling the wind against his face and naked chest, a sharp northerly wind he hadn't been aware of until that moment.

The wildfire was less than a mile behind them. Coming fast through the densely packed timberland, given impetus by the gusting wind.

FIFTY-ONE

Running, Regina saw that Steve Hannigan was one of the men standing beside the wrecked locomotive, and a sense of relief started to move through her. But it lasted for only a second, because then she realized Jim was the man lying motionless on the ground to one side with blood streaking his face and head.

Dead, she thought. He's dead.

She kept on running, stumbling now because her legs were weak, and fought her way past Steve and the other men and fell to her knees beside Jim. Stared at his bloody, ravaged face. And saw little red frothy bubbles coming out of both nostrils, heard the faint, liquid inhale-exhale of air.

He wasn't dead; he was *breathing*.

She made an involuntary sound in her throat that was half laugh, half sob. From the moment she'd heard the couplings break loose and the wild, grinding crash begin, she'd been sure both Steve and Jim would be killed, and when the coaches had come to a stop and she'd lifted herself off Ed Staggers and gotten outside and seen what was left of the locomotive, she'd been even more convinced of it.

The sense of relief stayed with her this time as she lifted Jim's wrist, felt for the pulse. Strong. There was blood in his mouth; he could suffocate if it backed up in his throat and lungs. She turned his head and pushed him gently onto his side, wiped away some of the blood with the back of her hand. Then she felt his body, touched the area around the wound on his head. Concussion, maybe a skull fracture. Possible internal injuries.

No. Just a concussion, just that.

She became aware then of the movement and noise around her. People swarming confusedly. Jack Bennett's little girl wailing in pain from her broken arm. Martha Staggers praying aloud. Women crying something about guns and other weapons. Men shouting, men talking in loud, urgent voices.

"Everybody keep calm, stay together!"

"We can't run fast enough on foot. The fire'll be here pretty soon; it'll explode those munitions."

"Forestry people have got to have fire lines set up by now. They'll be out at least two miles this side of Springwood."

"There's a logging road crosses the tracks a little more than a mile from here. If we can get to that . . ."

"Stay together, stay calm!"

"Another air tanker flew over a while back; the pilot must have seen us and radioed in. When we don't show, they'll come looking for us; they'll come on that logging road."

"All right, for God's sake, let's move."

"Everybody move out downtrack! Stay together, don't run, save your strength!"

Regina stood up. Most of the villagers, obeying orders, were hurrying frantically away from the locomotive in a tight pack spread across the rails and ties. She saw Logan and Adcock pick up Ed Staggers from where they had put him down on the ground, Linscott helping them. Saw beyond them, for the first time with recognition, the weapons that were scattered across the east slope—small guns, huge ugly guns, other things she couldn't identify. War things, war weapons. She didn't understand, and the feeling of unreality touched her mind again. The smoke-tainted wind rippled her damp hair, made her shiver.

Steve and Tyrell and Burt Evans were coming up to where she was standing beside Jim. Steve caught her arm as the other two bent to lift Jim between them. His face was battered, soot-blackened; there were burns and cuts and scrapes on his bare chest and shoulders, on both arms. Ravaged too, just like Jim. But he looked . . . strong. Strong.

"You all right, Regina?"

"Yes. Yes."

"Better catch up with the others; we'll take care of Jim."

"No, I want to help with him."

"There's nothing you can do—"

"I've got to stay with him, Steve."

Something flickered in his eyes, seemed to deaden them for an instant. He said, "Okay," and turned immediately to help Tyrell and Evans.

Supporting Jim, the four of them hurried awkwardly down the track in the wake of the others. The forward group of townspeople began to disappear around the curve in the tracks, and for a moment it seemed to Regina—more unreality—as if they were simply vanishing, walking into a void or off the edge of a precipice. She thought of the word *lemmings* and shivered again and turned her head to look back at the wrecked and abandoned train.

At the pale smoky fire glow looming higher, closer in the dawn sky.

FIFTY-TWO

In the first few seconds after he regained consciousness, Zacharias didn't know where he was.

He was groggy, his mind fogged with pain. There were sharp pulses of agony in his right shoulder when he moved. Something under and around him crunched and snapped, gouged at his body like poking fingers. He raised up on his left elbow, and there was more snapping and crunching, more pain. When his vision finally cleared, he was looking at ferns and dry underbrush, the short rocky bank of a dry creek, the mossy trunks of trees. Seeing them clearly because there was dusky light in the sky now—it was almost dawn.

He realized then how quiet it was.

Not just quiet—a hushed, eerie stillness. No sounds anywhere except for the rustling whisper of wind and a faint, distant thrumming.

The underbrush was clumped up behind his head, draped over part of his body; he was half-buried in it. He swept it away with his left arm, sat up and slid around onto his knees, biting down hard against the stabbing pain in his shoulder. He was at the bottom of the slope on the east side of the tracks. He stared up the slope. The train was there, on and off the rails, broken into three pieces—the boiler hadn't blown after all, something else had torn up the locomotive and caused the wreck. And the whole area was deserted, the people gone.

He smelled smoke again—and saw the fire raging toward him from the north. It was the goddamn *fire* that was making that distant thrumming noise.

Struggling, he got up on his feet. His right arm hung stiffly at his side; he knew without thinking about it that the shoulder had been dislocated in the long tumbling fall down the slope. But his legs were all right; he could walk and he could run.

He scrambled up toward the tracks. Pain cut at him with every step, but he made himself ignore it, didn't let it slow him down. Half of the ordnance from the derailed boxcar was scattered over the slope, and as he dodged through it, he thought that he had to have a gun: he'd lost the Woodsman inside the engine. He wouldn't stand a chance of making it out of Springwood and out of these mountains without a weapon, not hurt the way he was.

Making it out of Springwood. Jesus Christ, he had to make it to Springwood first—get across those fire lines somehow. Two miles on foot at least, maybe as much as four, with that son of a bitch fire up there roaring toward him, with the ordnance set to go off as soon as the blaze got close . . .

Stay cool, stay cool.

He got a tight hold on his mind, blocked out everything except the situation here and now. He was halfway up the slope, and he shifted his eyes back and forth as he ran, looking for a handgun. Saw a cluster of the Government-issue .45 automatics off to the left, went over and bent down and scooped one of them up in his left hand. Now he needed a clip; there had to be ammunition clips around here somewhere—and his eyes picked out a broken ammunition crate twenty yards behind him, up the slope, black clips spilled out in the grass near it like toppled dominoes. He ran back that way, caught one up, then plunged upward again.

When he got to level ground beside the tracks he slowed long enough to wedge the .45 under his stiffened arm, drive the clip into the butt, and shove the automatic down inside his pants at the belt. The sound of the fire was louder in his ears, punctuated by barely audible cracklings. He threw a look that way. Smoke rolled toward him in long, billowing columns. He could see flames high up on one of the ridges, a faded yellow-red in the morning light, no more than half a mile away.

He grabbed his right arm, held it tight against his body, and ran past the locomotive and then headlong down the center of the tracks.

FIFTY-THREE

Moving at a slowed trot behind the rest of the fleeing villagers, Hannigan and eleven of the other men carried Staggers and Maxon in three-man, five-minute shifts: carry, rest, carry, rest. The men in each team stood shoulder to shoulder, supporting one of the unconscious men across their bodies on forward-curved arms, the way you would carry an armload of heavy firewood. Doing it that way let them run straight ahead instead of having to move sideways.

Hannigan had just been relieved again and had come down off the ties to the packed earth of the right-of-way. His arms and legs were leaden from the constant strain, fingers and toes tingling with numbness that he couldn't quite flex away. Fatigue made him light-headed, giddy. They were all near exhaustion, functioning on bare reserves of energy, and their pace had slowed steadily during the past few minutes. Ahead he could see people staggering, swaying drunkenly. Some of them had fallen but had gotten up again on their own or with help. Men supported and half-dragged wives and older children, carried the younger kids. Silent, all of them—no cries, not even audible whimpers from the children. There were no sounds at all except the wind and their shuffling steps and panting breaths.

How far had they come? Had to be nearly a mile, which meant it was no more than thirty minutes since they'd left the wrecked train. It seemed to Hannigan they had been running for hours; his sense of time was distorted. But the fire hadn't reached the munitions yet—any minute now, but not yet—and they were out of the immediate danger zone of the explosion. Still, he knew that when the remaining boxcar finally did blow, the explosion would hurl fire and shrapnel for considerable distances, could start a new blaze close behind them, on either side of them. They wouldn't even be near safety until they got to the logging road, and then it would all depend on where the fire fighters were, how fast the fire spread after the explosion, how much strength they had left.

Above a series of sawtooth ridges to the east, the sky was stained a deepening ruby color streaked with purples and golds and hazed by smoke. The grayness overhead and to the west was tinted with faded blue, but down here the light was uncertain, made murky by tree shadows. Hannigan dragged an arm across his sweating face, squinted past the straggled line of townspeople. He could make out a downward left-hand turn far ahead; where they were now, the tracks ran in an even line. He tried to remember exactly where the logging road crossed the right-of-way, couldn't seem to visualize it or the terrain near it in his mind. No particular landmarks in this area. Just timberland, unrelieved wilderness crowding in on both sides.

He shifted his gaze to Regina. She was still trotting along behind the men who were carrying Maxon. She had been there the whole time, not trying to help any more because she didn't have the strength and she'd only been getting in the way, just keeping a kind of vigil. *I've got to stay with him, Steve.* Meaning only now, here, until this ordeal was over one way or the other? Or meaning more than that, telling him consciously or unconsciously that she had made her decision between them, and Maxon was the one she'd chosen? Dully, Hannigan thought he knew the answer. But he didn't feel anything yet; he had been drained of the capacity for emotion. Later, if they made it through, he would feel a great deal—he would feel too much.

Seconds passed, minutes passed. The other teams began to falter, to call for relief. Instead of going to help with Maxon this time, Hannigan ran ahead and joined Linscott and Oldaker on Ed Staggers. He got between the other two, took the old man under the hips. Staggers' face was gray, waxy; he looked dead. But his chest moved faintly; breath rattled in his throat. The bandaged wound in his upper chest was soaked with blood—dried, drying, and fresh.

He's not going to make it, Hannigan thought.

Then he thought: Hang on, hang on. Talking mutely to Staggers, and to himself and the others, too.

Minutes, more and more minutes. Carry. Rest. Still no explosion. Into the downward curve, out of it into another straight and the same empty, silent green and brown wilderness. He lost all track of time and distance. Began to feel detached, as if a sentient part of him were standing off at a distance and watching the movements of his body with an objective eye. Watching and waiting for him, for all of them, to begin dropping from exhaustion by ones and twos . . .

There was a buzzing, hammering noise in the sky to the south.

Hannigan pulled his eyes up from the ground beneath his feet, saw others do the same. Everyone slowed to a walk, to a breathless standstill as the noise grew louder and the silvery body of another air tanker appeared, flying very low, flying straight at them. It reached a point above them within seconds, and people waved feverishly, unnecessarily: the pilot saw them, all right, he couldn't help but see them at that low altitude. And when he flew overhead he dipped one wing to tell them he knew they were there.

The coming of the plane seemed to animate the villagers, to shore up their flagging strength and hope. They were all thinking the same things Hannigan was, saying them to each other: the Forestry people had sent the plane out to look for them when they hadn't arrived at the fire lines; the pilot would radio back that they were all on foot now; ground vehicles would be dispatched immediately onto that logging road. The road couldn't be far ahead of them, *if they could only get to that road.*

And they were all running again.

FIFTY-FOUR

Zacharias didn't slow up when the air tanker went over, didn't even look at it. The chemicals it was carrying weren't going to keep the munitions from blowing, weren't going to stop the fire from spreading out behind him. He kept waiting for that goddamn ordnance to go and it kept on not happening. Maybe the wind had shifted or slackened; he couldn't tell, he didn't know anything about wind currents. All he knew or cared about was that the heat of the fire hadn't reached the train yet—and the longer it didn't, the less slim his chances were.

He rounded a turn in the tracks, still pounding down the center of the ties. His breath came in ragged gasps. There was agony in his dislocated shoulder, in his legs and chest. He'd stumbled and fallen a couple of times, lost the .45 once and had to waste several seconds looking for it and then getting it shoved down inside his belt again. But for all of that, he'd managed so far to maintain a steady running pace for what had to have been a mile or better.

Through a film of sweat he saw that the tracks ahead were still empty. The people from the village must have had a big jump on him; he was running faster than they'd be able to with the women and kids. He didn't know what he'd do if he did catch up to them. Hang back and follow them to the fire lines—at a pace that might be too slow? Run through them, past them—and let them know he was alive, not dead back there, and run the risk of hitting the fire lines blind? Go off into the woods, try to follow along even with them, out of sight—and risk getting himself lost?

He just didn't know. He couldn't think straight, couldn't plan ahead any more; his head didn't want to work right again. It was the pain and the near-exhaustion that were doing it now, and the way things had kept on getting worse, more complicated, more and more foreign to his experience. He was having crazy little mental flashes, too. Lila and the kid. How they looked when they dressed up in the same clothes, wore their hair the same way. The sailboat he was building, and the clean salt smell when he was out sailing on the harbor. The look and feel of a satchel of money and the look and feel of Lila beside him in the night.

He kept up the grueling pace until he was into another curve, halfway out of it. Then he could feel himself slowing down, starting to wobble, like a car engine firing on half its cylinders. His legs were rubbery, full of sharp stinging needles. Blood roared in his ears. He had to rest for a few seconds; he knew if he didn't he would collapse.

Gasping, he pulled up and bent over at the waist and sucked air through his open mouth. Some of the tightness in his chest, some of the weakness in his legs eased after a minute. When the hammering in his ears quit he forced himself to move again. But he wasn't running any more, he was only staggering forward in a loose-gaited jog.

Christ, how much farther to those fire lines? How much longer before—

And the ordnance blew.

Even though he was thinking about it happening, waiting for it, the sudden echoing blast threw him off stride. The ties under his feet seemed to ripple from concussion; the shadowy morning turned match-flame bright. There were more explosions, an immediate chain of them, like bombs falling on an artillery target. He regained his balance, wheeled around.

The sky behind him was raining fire.

FIFTY-FIVE

Regina saw the logging road appear ahead of them seconds before the explosion.

They were just coming around a gradual bend, and one of the men down in the front line had let out a weak shout. She'd lifted her head, blinking, and people were pointing, calling out, and when she'd run a little farther behind the men who were carrying Jim, there it was, less than a hundred yards away—a rutted brown line that bisected a shallow clearing to the east, crossed the tracks, and vanished through the trees to the west.

It was empty, there was no sign of fire-fighting crews or vehicles. But they'd come pretty soon; the belief that they would come and the belief that getting to the road meant safety at last had kept all of the villagers going for the past few minutes. Still, she'd been afraid her legs and the rest of her body would give out before they reached the road, afraid that if she did collapse she would not be able to get up again. Now, seeing the road down there, she knew she had enough strength left to—

And that was when the explosion happened.

Convulsively, she threw her arms up and locked them over her ears to shut out the awful roaring noise of it. There were cries all along the tracks, people slowing, turning as she did to look to the north. Black smoke and swirling flame blanketed the sky above the treetops. More smoke and pellets and arrows of fire hurtled toward them, out away from them on both sides, as the sound of the explosion diminished into a series of muted whistling detonations.

None of the falling fire reached them, just wispy vanguards of smoke. But flames landed on trees no more than a thousand yards away, set them instantly ablaze; fire began to race through the dry top branches, sending up cascades of sparks and cinders. The air turned hot and foul and made Regina cough and then gag.

Someone grabbed her, whirled her around. Steve. She sagged against him, let him pull her away, because her legs just didn't want to work any more on their own. Her mind was jumbled. She couldn't get enough air into her lungs, and she could barely see for the haze of smoke in front of her eyes and the haze of fatigue behind them.

She had a dim awareness of the others running, veering off the tracks, toward the logging road on the east. The whistling explosions had stopped; she heard only the humming crackle of fire a long way off, like the sound of the sea inside a conch shell.

Then they were on the logging road, stumbling down the ruts with the fire racing after them—and nothing ahead of them but emptiness. . . .

FIFTY-SIX

As soon as Zacharias saw the fire raining down behind him, he forgot all about the pain in his shoulder and legs and chest and broke into a hard forward run. He ran with his head down and his neck muscles bunched, telling himself the fallout wouldn't reach this far, half-expecting flames to drop down on him. But it didn't happen, didn't happen—and seconds or minutes later there were no more explosions, just the distant intermittent gunfire noise of erupting ammunition. Then he could hear the malignant thrumming of the blaze, the muffled *whoosh* of tree branches igniting; but he didn't look back. He didn't want to know how close the fire was settling in on him.

Choking gray-black smoke eddied around him, clogged his nostrils, burned in his throat. He ran blind for more seconds or minutes, tripped on a warped tie as he came out ahead of the curling tendrils extending low over the tracks, and sprawled out sideways onto one of the rails. Agony burst through his right side. He clawed himself upright, plunged through another turn and into the next straight stretch.

He didn't see the road until he was almost on top of it.

When he did see it—a horizontal line crossing the tracks east to west, blurred by sweat and tears—he slowed reflexively into a weaving, splayfooted trot. His mind stuttered, released thoughts. Take the road? Maybe one of the directions led out to where the fire lines were, maybe that was where the townspeople had gone. But which one? If he took the wrong one he might trap himself. It could be that both of them led to the fire lines—but it could also be that neither one did and the villagers were still up ahead, following the tracks.

His decision was less conscious than compulsive: he kept on going, past the road and straight down the ties.

The sounds of the fire, his breathing, his shoes slapping against wood and earth blended into a muted throbbing pulse. The pain dulled until finally he had no awareness of it at all. His mind began to go blank, to turn into a kind of gray void shot through with flashes and streaks of color . . .

There were two men ahead of him.

All at once he was seeing two men come up onto the tracks fifty yards ahead of him.

The visual perception was like an electric shock.

The color-streaked grayness evaporated; the hammering in his ears diminished; all his senses came rushing back. He slowed into a lurching walk, blinked and pawed at his eyes. The men were running toward him now, and he could see that they were both wearing yellow hard-hat helmets and carrying walkie-talkie units clipped to their belts.

Fire fighters, the fire lines.

Zacharias came to a stop. His lungs were like knives in his chest. He stood there swaying, sucking smoky air, and inside him was a thin wild laughter that didn't quite come out because he had no breath for it.

By the time the two fire fighters got to him he could think again; he was starting to regain a semblance of control over himself. They could tell from the way he was clutching his right arm that it was injured, so one of them reached out to grasp his left arm gently, steady him. He let the man do it. He didn't want their hands on him, not with the gun inside his waistband, but he was too weak and too full of pain to fend the guy off.

The other one said, "Jesus," in an awed way. He was looking at Zacharias' face. Then he said, "Take it easy, mister, we'll have you out of here pretty quick."

Zacharias looked back to the north. Smoke curled along the tracks, between the walls of trees. He could see flames dancing skyward above the gray pall, but none of them were close yet.

The first fire fighter said, "What happened to the other people? They somewhere back there?"

He pulled his head around. The stabbing agony in his lungs had lessened; his respiration had slowed enough so that he could talk. "No," he managed in a hoarse, scratchy voice. "Thought they were ahead of me."

"They must have taken the Number 6 road up there," the first one said to his partner.

The partner nodded grimly, and the one holding his arm began leading him hurriedly downtrack. His legs were wobbly, full of shooting pains, but he could still walk all right. Walk all right and think all right—those were the things that mattered right now.

"What were those explosions a little while ago?" the second fire fighter asked him. "Sounded like a war going on. Sounded like Nam, for God's sake."

"Don't know. Listen, where're you taking me?"

"There's another logging road through the trees to the west," the first guy said. "We were sent out to check the tracks along here."

"Anybody else with you?"

"No."

"You come on foot?"

"Jeep. Don't worry, we'll get you clear."

"To where?" But he was thinking: Jeep, jeep.

"Command post set up a mile south of here," the second one said. "I'll call ahead for an ambulance."

"I don't need an ambulance."

"You need one, mister."

They were leading him down off the right-of-way now, into the woods, and the second guy was unhooking the walkie-talkie unit from his belt. That meant Zacharias couldn't wait; the time was right now. He pulled out of the other one's grasp, stepped back and dragged the .45 out from under his ragged sweater with his left hand. The two of them stopped and started to turn, froze when they saw the gun and stood staring at it, wide-eyed.

"What the hell?" the second one said.

"You do what I tell you, you won't get hurt."

"What's the idea of that gun?"

"Shut up. Put the walkie-talkie away."

The guy hesitated, exchanged a look with his partner.

"Put it away or I'll blow your head off."

"He means it, Chet," the first one said warningly.

Tight-faced, watching the gun, the guy named Chet hooked the unit back onto his belt.

"All right," Zacharias said. "Lead the way to the jeep."

They didn't give him any argument. They just turned and plowed ahead through the trees and a heavy ground cover of ferns and fallen logs and dry brush, through thin wisps of foglike smoke. More smoke undulated overhead, shutting out part of the morning sky. Zacharias could hear the faint murmuring crackle of the fire, but there was more than enough time for him to make it out of here with their jeep. His luck was holding after all, despite the shape he was in and despite the fire and the goddamn ordnance. He'd make it now. He'd make it with just a little more luck.

Up ahead the second guy called over his shoulder, "I don't know who you are, mister, but throwing down on us with that gun puts you in big trouble."

"Shut up."

"You're going to leave us here, is that it? Steal our jeep and leave us stranded here?"

"Shut up, I said!"

The guy shut up. Past him, through the trees, Zacharias saw part of the logging road and part of the jeep. They'd already turned the machine around so that it was pointing back to the south. The woods and the ground cover thinned out, and half a minute later they came out onto the road.

The two fire fighters stopped beside the jeep. The

second one said, "What happens now? You going to shoot us?"

"Keep prodding me, you'll find out."

The first guy put a hand on his partner's arm. "Easy, Chet."

"You listen to him, Chet." Zacharias went over by the driver's door and glanced inside. The key was in the ignition. "Okay," he said, pointing to the rear seat, "both of you throw those walkie-talkies in back here."

No hesitation this time. The two of them unhooked their units and tossed them in.

"Now go around the other side and head down the road, off on the side. Don't look back here; just keep walking."

They did that, watching him until they were clear of the jeep, then putting their eyes to the front. Zacharias waited until they'd gone twenty yards before he climbed inside and laid the gun down on the seat beside him. He turned the ignition key and hit the starter. The motor roared immediately, and the one guy, Chet, looked back over his shoulder, but they both kept on walking. Zacharias reached over clumsily with his left hand, shifted out of neutral into low, and popped the clutch.

The rear tires spun on the hard dirt, caught traction. The jeep jumped forward, and he had to fight the wheel with his one hand to get it straightened out. The two fire fighters threw themselves off the road into the undergrowth as he shot past them with the engine screaming in low gear. He managed to shift into second but almost lost control of the jeep when he did. Leave it in second then; the transmission would stand the strain.

He looked up into the mirror. The two guys were

back on the road, running after him. Maybe he should have put both their lights out back there, he thought. They knew what he looked like, that was one thing, and they'd get to the command post in twenty minutes or so. But if any of the people from the village made it through, they'd be able to describe him just as well—and the double murder of a couple fire fighters would sure as Christ make the cops concentrate more on catching him than on getting everybody out of the area and controlling the fire. Twenty minutes was plenty of time for him to drive clear of the command post, find a state or county road and then a place to hole up until he could get in touch with Lila and have her drive up to get him.

The jeep jounced and rattled on the rutted road. Every jolt sent white-hot pain through his dislocated shoulder, but he was used to agony now; it hadn't stopped him from functioning before and he wouldn't let it stop him now. He kept one eye on the odometer because when he got near the command post he'd have to slow down. He couldn't just barrel through the area; he didn't know what was there and he didn't want to alert anybody that something was going down.

The odometer had clicked off seven-tenths of a mile when a sharp left-hand curve loomed ahead. He tapped the brakes, slid into the turn, started out of it—

And there were two cars—two county sheriff's cruisers—sitting across the road up ahead.

Surprise and disbelief turned him rigid, made him lift his foot off the accelerator. The road was narrow at that point, with trees and undergrowth bunched up close on both sides, and the cars were angled one behind the other so that all the road surface was blocked. He could see tan-uniformed deputies crouched down behind the cars and off in the woods, three or four of them.

Waiting for him, *waiting* for him.

But how could they have known—

The walkie-talkies. Jesus Christ, the fire fighter named Chet must have opened the Send button on his unit while they were moving through the trees; that was why he'd called out about the gun and stealing the jeep.

Stupid! Too exhausted, too screwed up mentally to foresee the possibility—stupid, stupid!

There was no way to get through the cruisers, no way to get around them. Desperately Zacharias jammed his foot down on the brake pedal, held tight to the wheel until the jeep began to grind to a slewing sidewise stop, and then let go of it and snatched up the .45 from the seat. When the jeep jolted into the first cruiser, he shoved down on the door handle with his gun hand and threw himself out. Hit the roadbed rolling, the burst of pain in his shoulder half-blinding him. He came up onto his knees, the sounds of shouting in his ears, and fired a quick shot, not trying to hit any of them, just trying to buy himself enough time to scramble into the trees.

Knowing all the while he'd never make it.

Knowing it was all over, all over—his luck had finally run out.

FIFTY-SEVEN

Hannigan, his right arm tight around Regina's shoulders, took a quick look behind him as they stumbled down the logging road behind the other villagers. The fire hadn't spread near them yet, but the tops of the trees two hundred yards back were obscured by billowing smoke. Off to the west, beyond the railroad tracks, colorless flames boiled across the nearest ridge.

He swiveled his head to the front again. Regina was coughing in spasms that shook her body; his own breath wheezed in his throat, exploded out of his mouth in staccato gasps. The smoke and the dense configuration of the evergreens cast deep hazy shadows over the road; it was like running through a dark, blurred nightmare—the kind in which you run and run and never get anywhere.

Ahead, people were doubled over and weaving erratically; people were falling and being hauled back up by neighbors and relatives. There was panic in all of them again, but it was driving them onward, giving impetus to their enervated bodies.

Where were the fire fighters?

Where were the relief vehicles?

Come on, come on, *come on!*

Hannigan's foot hit sideways in one of the ruts and his legs buckled and he went down; his weight pulled Regina down with him. He shoved up on one knee, and for an instant he was frozen there, couldn't raise himself onto his feet again. Then his muscles worked convulsively and he was standing—he dragged Regina up by one arm and folded her against him again.

Ran with her again.

The smoke got thicker. The harsh, superheated air gusted against the back of his neck.

More people fell; the men carrying Maxon almost dropped him.

One, two, three more air tankers flew low overhead to the west.

And when the roar of the planes faded, Hannigan heard something else: whining sounds, mechanical sounds, *automobile* sounds.

Jeeps and trucks, coming on the other side of the bend up ahead.

Coming, coming.

God.

The forward group of townspeople stopped running. Some of them fell to their knees; others began waving their arms in a kind of frenzy. The engine sounds increased in volume, and finally a jeep appeared out of the smoke haze at the bend, a stake-sided truck, another truck, an ambulance—a small convoy of vehicles plowing toward them, halting. Helmeted fire fighters and volunteer medics spilled out, rushed forward.

Hannigan felt himself begin to tremble with fatigue and the release of tension. Heard Regina in her own relief making half-hysterical hiccoughing sounds. Walking faster, he plodded ahead of her. In front of them the fire fighters shouted orders to one another, asked people if there was anybody missing, anybody else coming. Villagers climbed into the trucks or were boosted into them by the men; medics took charge of Maxon and Staggers and carried them to the ambulance. To Hannigan, it all seemed to be happening in a kind of fuzzy motion that was both fast and slow, as if his mind were constantly changing speeds to create a photographic illusion.

When they neared the first jeep Regina pulled away from him. She wanted to go to the ambulance, he understood that, and he didn't try to hold on to her. He just let her go.

Just let her go.

Linscott and Oldaker were already slumped in the back of the first jeep; Hannigan collapsed into the front passenger seat and sat there staring blankly at the smoke funneling down the road. He wanted to close his eyes, didn't do it because he felt he would pass out the instant he did.

Engines roared again: the rearmost vehicles were loaded full and beginning to reverse out. A heavy-set fire fighter with a handkerchief tied over his face slid in beside Hannigan, glanced over at him as he waited his turn to move.

"Man," the fire fighter said, "we couldn't have cut it any closer. That fire'll be here in another few minutes."

Hannigan managed a nod.

"Tell you the truth, we were afraid you wouldn't make it this far." The fire fighter shook his head. "We gave you up for dead more than once this morning."

Hannigan found his voice just before they started to move. "So did we," he said.

EPILOGUE

Maxon, his head swathed in bandages, lay in bed in the private hospital room and stared up at the white ceiling without seeing it. The hospital was in Redding, the town to which they had all been evacuated that morning by helicopter and ground vehicle. It was night now, a little before nine o'clock. A doctor had told him where he was and what the time was when he'd awakened a few minutes ago.

The doctor had also told him most of what had happened after the rod on the Baldwin had let go and he'd been knocked unconscious. That he'd been the only one seriously injured in the train derailment, and how the villagers had run the last mile and a half to the fire line, carrying him and Ed Staggers. That they had all miraculously made it to safety with no casualties; even Staggers, though he was still in critical condition, had survived and was given an even chance to live. That the lean stranger had somehow made it to the fire lines, too, alone, and stolen a jeep there, and been shot and critically wounded in a county police roadblock; he was under guard here in this same hospital, but had not yet been identified or questioned about the explosion at the mill, the apparent death of Henry Johnston, the theft of the munitions. That the Forestry Service fire fighters had managed to save most of Springwood and were hoping to contain the fire sometime that evening.

He was thinking about all those things—but mostly he was thinking about his own actions in the locomotive cab before the crash. His memory of those hours on the train was dim, dreamlike, as if he had watched the things that had happened instead of living them. Part of the reason might be the head blow he'd taken, the concussion the doctor told him he had. But part of it, too, was a kind of defense mechanism: his mind shying away from what he understood now was a lunatic time of foolishness and reckless misjudgment.

Because he had been wrong in nearly everything he'd felt and done during that time. Wrong about the Baldwin's capacity to withstand the constant strain of a wide-open throttle. Wrong about the importance of overpowering the stranger, disarming him. Wrong about himself. It was strange in a terrible way how you could be so sure of yourself in a situation, and then have the certainty shattered by the unexpected, and finally wake up, half a day later, to the realization of how irrational you'd really been.

What he felt most of all now, lying there, was an emotion brand-new to him.

He felt ashamed.

He moved his head around gingerly on the pillow and looked through the window adjacent to his bed. The sky was a deep black, pinholed here and there with stars. But there were clouds up there, too, dark and restless, massing to the east and beginning to scud westward. Rain clouds—it was going to rain tonight for the first time in five months. Maybe it would be a brief shower, but maybe, too, it would last long enough to mark the end of the drought.

The irony didn't escape him: either way, the rain would be coming one day too late.

For him, for all the people of Logspur—one day too late.

He was still watching the movement of the clouds when the door opened and someone came inside. He turned his head then, saw that it was Regina, and blinked at her in the pale light from the nightstand lamp. She looked all right. Weary, hollow-eyed, but otherwise all right. She wore a faded dress that somebody must have given her, and her blonde hair was washed clean and brushed straight down from a center part. There was a small, grave smile on her mouth as she came across to the bed.

"Hi," she said.

"Hi."

"How do you feel?"

"Sick. Doctor tells me I've got a concussion."

"Yes, but it's not serious. The X-rays they took were negative." She sat down on the metal chair beside the bed, touched his arm briefly, then folded her hands in her lap.

Maxon said, "I know most of what happened, from the doctor. We're all lucky to be alive."

She nodded.

"The train wreck was my fault," he said. "Did Hannigan tell you that?"

"No. He didn't say anything about it."

"He was one of the men who helped carry me out, wasn't he?"

"Yes."

Wrong about Hannigan, too.

"Anyway," Regina said, "it doesn't matter about the wreck. Not now."

"It matters."

"No, it doesn't. We're all safe, that's the important thing."

"I could have killed us all," he said.

"Jim . . ."

Maxon ran his tongue over cracked lips. "It's all

right; I'm not feeling sorry for myself. I'm just stating a fact."

She was silent for a time, watching him. "Jim," she said finally, "what happens next?"

"Next?"

"With you. With us."

"I don't know," he said. "I'm not the same person I was twenty-four hours ago. I guess none of us are. I learned a lot of things last night, but I'm not sure yet what any of them mean."

"Are you still so bitter about your leg?"

"I can't forget about it, Regina—I'll never forget about it. But maybe I can learn to live with it."

"If the dispatcher's job in Eureka is still open, would you reconsider taking it?"

"Maybe. I think I might."

"I'm glad."

He turned his head away from her and looked again at the scudding black-edged clouds beyond the window. Then at length he looked back to her and said, "About us—we have to talk about us."

Another nod. "But we don't have to do it now."

"Yes, we do. Right now."

"If you feel up to it."

"Because it's something we should've done a long time ago. I know that now."

"I'm glad about that, too."

"For both our sakes," he said.

"Yes," she said. "For both our sakes."

Alone in the room he had been given at the Redding Lodge, Hannigan sat in darkness and listened to the whisper of his own thoughts.

After they had treated him at the hospital and released him, and he had been driven here, he'd slept for more than ten hours. But he didn't feel much better now than he had before going to bed. He was still exhausted, and there was still a vague tension in him. And a kind of emptiness, too, because he had already accepted the truth about Regina.

She was going to stay with Maxon.

He'd known that for certain when she went to the ambulance on the logging road, and he had had all the confirmation he needed later on when she made no effort to see or talk to him at the hospital or at the lodge. He had considered seeking her out tonight, but there would have been no point in it; it would have been too painful. Better not to see her again. Better for him, better for her, too.

Would she be happy with Maxon? Maybe she would; it all depended on whether or not he remained the bitter man Hannigan had known the past six months, the foolish man he'd seen in the locomotive cab that morning. Either way, Hannigan would never see him again—and never hate him any more, either. The hate had died sometime during their agonizing run to the logging road; all the destructive violence of those morning hours had, at last, purged the destructive and violent emotions inside him.

Would he ever get over Regina? No. But time would dull the ache for her, and when enough time had passed he would not think about her very much. Meanwhile, he would occupy himself with trying to rebuild his material existence. Find a new location somewhere in these northern mountains in which to settle, in which to construct a new woodbutcher's cabin and stock it with new personal possessions. Reconstruct the history of short-line railroading in

Northern California, too; he could do that well enough from memory, since he had written less than half the book prior to yesterday.

He had known contentment once living alone, being alone. Someday, maybe, he would find it again.

It was stuffy in the room, and the raw burned skin beneath the bandages on his bare shoulder and chest and hands itched from perspiration. He got up and crossed to the window, opened it. The warm night breeze came in against his face. He stood there for a time, letting the breeze dry the sweat on him. Then he turned to start back for the chair.

There was a soft rapping on the door.

He frowned slightly, went over and opened it—and the ache in him sharpened, made his mouth and throat dry.

"Regina," he said.

"Hello, Steve."

He stepped back so she could enter. Closed the door and pivoted to the table nearby and switched on the lamp. When he turned back to her she was watching him with her eyes dark and an odd expression on her face that he couldn't quite read.

He said, "Maxon must be okay or you'd still be at the hospital."

"He's going to be okay, yes."

The way she said that carried more meaning than the obvious one, as if she were telling him that Maxon would be all right emotionally as well as physically. Good. Good.

"I know why you're here," he said.

"Do you?"

"To tell me your decision. But you didn't have to come; I already know what it is."

"I don't think you do." She took a long breath, let it out slowly. "Jim and I have agreed to get a divorce," she said.

He had trouble believing it for a second. Because he wanted it so much, he was afraid it couldn't be true.

"We had a long talk at the hospital," Regina said. "We decided it would be the best thing for both of us."

"But I thought—" He broke off, started over. "You went with him in the ambulance this morning, stayed at the hospital all day. I was sure you'd made up your mind to stay with him."

"He's still my husband and he was badly hurt. I *had* to be with him. And I had to talk to him before I saw you."

The ache in Hannigan was something different now, like a kind of painful joy. He just looked at her, embraced her with his eyes.

"He's going to find himself now," she said, "but he'll be able to do it without me. It's been over between us for a long time, and we both knew it, and tonight we finally admitted it to each other. He just doesn't need me any more."

"*I* need you," Hannigan said.

A little while later, the breeze blowing in through the open window sharpened and cooled and brought with it the smell of ozone.

And a little while after that, it began to rain.

**For More
Exciting Novels by
Award-Winning Author
Bill Pronzini**

The Alias Man
The Hangings
Firewind
With an Extreme Burning
Snowbound
The Stalker
Panic
Games
The Last Days of Horse-Shy Halloran
Quincannon
The Jade Figurine
Dead Run
Dago Red
Masques

Novels by Bill Pronzini & Marcia Muller
The Lighthouse
Beyond the Grave
Duo
Double

Visit us at www.speakingvolumes.us

www.ingramcontent.com/pod-product-compliance
Lightning Source LLC
Chambersburg PA
CBHW050514260626
47157CB00004B/1314